BLACK NANCY

BOOK I

Lennox Nelson

For my Beverly

CONTENTS

ACKNOWLEDGMENTS

Charles Madison, for being a true friend and brother to me. Daryl Nelson, for being my only witness of what was 2230. Ruby Garvin, for inspiring this story and giving me a home when I didn't have one, and crying, laughing, and drinking with me as we watched Tombstone for 12 straight hours! Troy Carter, for always accepting me for who I was without judgment and always being there when I needed you, I love you, Cuz! Kia Purifoy, for believing in the BLACK NANCY concept from the door, giving me the confidence to continue writing. Paris Brown, for representing my work in Atlanta. Roland Grimes Show. PYNKE Stiletto Vets (Sandra & Cyndi) for your tireless support in helping to bring BLACK NANCY to the masses. Rory Pullens and Nick & Mitra Lore, my mentors. The BLACK NANCY NATION, because of you she lives! Olivene Clavon, my mother on earth! Momma Bucci and John Bucci of John's Pork Shack-- John, thank you for always being a friend. Chucky Barry Jr., thank you for always being a true friend and gentleman.

Earl and Charming Nelson, for sacrificing much to help create the man I am today.

LENNOX NELSON

CHAPTER 1

Momma

My name is Ruby and I am thirteen years old. Surviving in the Deep South, some would call me a runaway slave, but we prefer to use the term former slave. Momma says she named me Ruby because, on the day I was born, my eyes shined like rubies in the sunlight. I am writing this chronicle to make sure my mother's story will be told true. Momma says that history is usually written by the side that wins a conflict, and may not always be told as accurately as it should have been. Well, this is my attempt to tell our story as it really happened.

We are freedom fighters in the slave states of America. The year, I believe, is somewhere around 1723 or 24-- it is hard to know for sure these days because we move constantly from plantation to plantation through many counties. We always try to stay two steps ahead of the slave catchers and random white folk along the roads. This is becoming increasingly difficult because of the large bounty that has been placed on momma's head; $1,000, dead or however they manage to bring us in. In spite of this, we attempt to help as many of our people as we can along the way.

Nancy, my momma, hates her name. I'm pretty sure she has another name, but I've only heard her say it once when I was a little girl and I can't remember it. Momma is a special kind of black woman. She was born a princess, the youngest child of Chief Yoruba, of the Ashanti Empire. She was and still is without equal, male or female, when it comes to using her sickles in battle.

Don't matter though because we're here now, in America and the crackas and every other living thing in these parts refer to her as Black Nancy, on account of if you meet her and you are her enemy, the last thing you see is the black of her skin. That always makes me feel proud to be her daughter.

We have been on the run since... well since as far back as I can remember. I recollect we started running when I was five; I know because that was the year I was supposed to stop sleeping in the same bed with momma. I had only been in the children's sleeping shack for a short time before me and momma left that place.

Momma was the Champion of all the fighting slaves on Captain Bishop's plantation. She never lost a battle. People would come from far and wide to see momma in the pit. I was born shortly after she arrived. She doesn't talk much about Poppa, whoever he may have been, but I can tell she really loved and missed him. Every time I asked her about him she would start to tell me but end up with tears in her eyes and then she would find something else to talk about.

It is sometimes hard to remember all of the details about that horrible place, the Bishop Plantation, I mean. Captain Bishop found momma in Africa and brought her back to train as a fighting slave. He was a large man, taller than most, black or white. I also have to admit, the Captain, was very handsome for a white man, charming too for a drunk, slave-beating, rapist. He was always extra nice to me, and the other young girls on the plantation. I remember when I was very little he would come into the sleeping shack, where me and the other small children slept. He would tuck us in one by one and give all of us (boys and girls) his special touch. Nine years is a long time but I am sure that is why momma decided it was time for us to leave Captain Bishop's plantation.

Momma says he was a member of a secret club down here in the South called The Society. The Society was a secret group of the wealthiest plantation owners in the slave states of America. From what momma tells me, these men are some of the nastiest and meanest crackas in all the South. They all trained fighting slaves, and once a month they would all gather at whatever plantation was designated to hold the fights. Momma says they would use these events to sow their nasty oats, and have something called an orgy, whatever that is.

Anyway, momma taught me to read and write when I was knee high to a grasshopper. She was taught how to read and write by Lisa, another slave on Captain Bishop's plantation. Lisa was the slave who taught Captain and Mrs. Bishop's badass kids their reading and math lessons. Every night after she was done taking care of Captain Bishop's kids, she would sneak over to our shack and teach momma everything she knew about reading, writing and math. Momma would question her all night about the white man's habits, as Lisa saw them. I would often ask momma why she needed to know that stuff. Momma would always say, "Baby, you must study your enemies, learn their habits, understand their ways."

We sleep by day, and travel by night, using the Freedom Stations for sanctuary. Momma teaches slaves to read everywhere we go. Sometimes there were as many as ten who were brave enough to sneak out and risk their lives just to learn from momma. To them she was sent from whatever God they believed in. Momma says she is building the army of our peoples' salvation, one slave at a time. My momma is the deadliest woman, black or white, in the south, but I know in my heart, we will not survive this. I will write our story until my eyes have been shut. I pray our story be found by one of our own people.

CHAPTER 2

First Kill

The wind was howling and the sparse dead leaves that clung to the branches of the dozen oak trees surrounding the shack we were waiting in, rattled with each gust. I could hear the sounds of crickets and night birds fill the night air. I was standing on an old wooden stool looking out of a broken window in the dingy, cobweb filled shack. The shack was situated only a few miles away from the Conway Plantation. Becoming bored, I turned to momma. "Momma! How long do I have to keep looking out of this stupid window? I'm tired of standing watch! We ain't seen hide nor hair of the man in weeks." *Uh-oh*, I thought to myself. She's got that scowl on her face, here it comes...

"First of all, Lil Miss, it's 'haven't' seen anyone in weeks! Did I teach you to speak like that? I think not! Secondly, just because we haven't seen him, doesn't mean he's stopped looking for us. Do you understand?"

"Yes, ma'am", I sighed, as I turned back to continue my watch. Momma calmed herself and walked over to me.

"Baby girl, we have to be ever vigilant. I have to be able to depend on you, and you, me." Momma smiled then kissed me lovingly on the forehead like she always did. "Right?", she asked.

I nodded and turned back to the window, sighing, "Yes, ma'am." Momma turned and walked toward the river rock fireplace on the back wall of the shack. She grabbed a slender green branch that was leaning on the hearth and began using it to stoke the fire. "Joshua, and whoever he's bringing, should be here soon. Keep a sharp eye now!" I strained my eyes trying to see through the darkness in all directions.

Without notice, the squeaky front door of the cabin swung open. Joshua, a large burly and bearded slave, wearing tattered clothes from the Conway Plantation, entered the shack with four other field hands with clothes in the same condition. Momma and me turned towards the squeaking shack door and she greeted them, "Welcome! Welcome! It does my heart glad to see so many of you! I am glad you all could make it. Have a seat and we'll get started." Momma quickly walked over to the small stack of firewood in the corner of the shack, she moved a few pieces of wood from the top of the pile, reached inside, and pulled a tattered bible from its hiding place. As she brought the bible to her breast, she turned and walked over to Joshua and the others, who sat cross-legged on the floor. Momma turned to me, "Ruby, a sharp eye out now." I turned my head sharply toward her, "I will momma!" I spun back to the window immediately to begin my watch again.

Momma opened the bible and passed it to Joshua. Joshua looked at the page, then looked up at momma and smiled. He nervously attempted to read. " 'The, the, though I, I, wa, walk thr , through the va, valley of de, death I, I, sh, sh, shall fe, fear no e, e, e'..." he looked up at momma for help. She smiled at him encouragingly and said. "Evil, the word is evil,

you know, like your Master Conway is evil?"
Joshua and the others chuckled. Momma smiled
reassuringly at Joshua, "That was some fine
reading Joshua, now let's give Missy a chance."
Joshua passed the bible to Missy, who was
seated beside him on the floor. Missy, a frail,
dark-skinned woman, took the book from Joshua
and read flawlessly.

" 'The Lord said, let there be light, and there
was light, and He saw that it was good.' "

I love watching momma teach people, it
makes me so proud to be called her daughter. I
was gloating so, about being her daughter that I
did not notice the thick-bearded, white man
creeping up behind me. I heard a twig break and
quickly turned back to look out of the window. I
saw nothing so I turned back to watch momma.
Suddenly, that white man snuck up behind me
and before I could even cry out, reached through
the broken window and violently snatched me
through what was left of the window frame. I
screamed as loud as I could, "Momma!
Momma!"

Momma ran to the window extending her
arms, but it was too late. The thick-bearded

white man held me in his powerful arms and covered my mouth with his hand so tightly that I could barely breath. Momma told me what happened after they grabbed me--

She jumped to her feet as well as Joshua, Missy, and the others. She whispered sternly, "Ya'll get back as best you can. I'm sorry, and good luck to you all."

But before she could stop him, Joshua opened the door and ran through it, trying to leave the field hands he had brought to the shack behind. He was immediately clubbed in the face by a muscular white man waiting outside of the shack door. He was hit so hard he flew back through the door and hit the floor of the shack like a piece of meat. She said his face was gruesomely bashed in.

All of the women were screaming, with the exception of momma. Momma ran over and slammed the door closed. Missy and the other women were paralyzed with fear so they just stood huddled together in a corner of the shack, trembling. Momma walked quickly over to them. "Now you listen, and you listen real good! Fear is a useless emotion! It is what has kept us in chains for all these years! We may not be able to control how they make us live, but we sure as hell can control how we die! Now, you choose, but I'm going out there to get my god-damn daughter!"

Momma turned and walked over to the fireplace, she removed some bricks from the hearth, reached inside and got her sickles from the opening. Before doing anything else, she dropped to her knees to pray. "Oh Heavenly Father, make me strong in the face of these devils. Make me swift in order to strike as many down as you see fit. Make me the instrument of your wrath. But know this, if something happens to my baby, it's gonna be me and you. In Jesus' name." She ran over to the fireplace and stomped the fire out.

Outside I could see the cabin go completely dark. I kicked and struggled to break free of the white man's grasp but he was too strong. I did manage to sink my teeth into his hand and yelled at the top of my lungs, "Momma, come get me!" The man regained control and covered my mouth once more. Momma said she heard me, so she knew in what direction I was. Momma crouched by the window I was pulled through and yelled, "Which one of you crackas is the head man out there?"

A tall white man with a long beard stepped out from the shadows of the woods. He spoke in a thick Southern drawl, "I'm in charge here, bitch! Mr. Conway don't take kindly to nigger bitches teaching other niggers to read! Hell, on top of that, that shit's against the goddamned law! So why don't you and the rest of them field hands just come out and make it easier on yourselves. If we have to come in there and gitcha, it'll be much more painful!" Momma yelled defiantly, "Then come get some, cracka!"

Joe Bob, the leader, motioned to two of his men to enter the shack. Cautiously the first man pulled a one shot pistol from his pants and cocked the hammer. The second man held a thick, oak wood club over his head as the first man opened the door of the shack. The door creaked loudly and then, as to cause confusion, both ran into the shack yelling wildly. The man with the pistol fired aimlessly into the darkness. The other man swung his club wildly into the air. The man with the pistol lifted his powder horn to the barrel of his pistol to reload.

He turned, facing the man with the club, and stated over-confidently, "Shit! That bitch didn't know who she was mess..." before he finished his sentence, momma sprung up from under the floorboards, cutting the man with the pistol's leg off from just below the knee. He fell to the floor in front of momma in agony holding the leg that was severed, screaming at the top of his lungs! Momma finished him with one swift downward swing of her sickle, beheading him. His head wobbled and rolled on the floor for a few moments next to his decapitated body. The whole thing reminded me of what the chickens did when they got their heads chopped off back on the old plantation.

Seeing his partner beheaded, the man with the club stood paralyzed in fear as he watched the one legged, headless body twitch on the floor. He slowly began to back away toward the door of the shack. Momma slowly approached him-- her face, hand, and sickle were covered in blood. That's when the rest of us outside heard the sound of metal and wood clashing. It stopped as suddenly as it began, dead silence followed. I began to cry because I knew they had killed momma.

The one called Joe Bob nervously called out to his men inside the shack, "Did you get her?" he snorted. The door of the shack swung open and the man with the club walked out normally. Joe Bob smiled and turned to the other men. "He got her, Boys!" Joe Bob and the three other men, including the one holding me, began to walk toward the man with the club, but his walking became labored. Joe Bob jovially called to him, "I know you didn't let that gal get a piece of you, boy?" Joe Bob and the others laughed, as they got closer to him. He turned, and that's when we all saw the whole right side of his head and face was missing. He fell to his knees as two of the men ran to assist him. Joe Bob peered into the darkness of the shack. He pointed his one shot pistol into it, and screamed angrily for momma. "Come out here bitch! I'm gonna tar and feather your niggra ass! Come out here right now!"

Joe Bob attempted to work up the courage to enter the shack. He looked over at the two men trying to help the dying man with the club. "Alright then, you two boys go in there and pull her nigger ass out here!" The two men looked down at the dead man with the club. They looked at one another, stood, and looked at Joe Bob with fear in their faces, then answered him in unison, "Piss on that!" Joe Bob frustrated, turned away from the shack and made sure his pistol was loaded. He faced back toward the shack and mustered all the courage he could and yelled, "Shit! Shit! Shit! Shit! I guess if you want something done, you gotta do it your god-damned self!"

Joe Bob cocked the hammer of his pistol and began to move toward the shack. He entered the shack quickly, jumping over Joshua's body. He saw the headless body of his man lying in a pool of his own blood. He looked around the shack very cautiously and realized that momma and the other women had escaped. He turned and quickly headed out the door, yelling, "Those bitches flew the coop!"

The men he left outside did not reply. "Hey! Did you boys here me?" Joe Bob walked out the door of the shack and found the remainder of his men dead on the ground. He walked over to the man's body, who was holding me. Momma intentionally rustled leaves on the ground behind him. He heard them and quickly turned raising his pistol. His hand trembled uncontrollably.

Momma walked out of the woods calmly towards Joe Bob and stopped in front of him. He closed his left eye to take aim at momma and said nervously, "You're one dead nig..." Before that cracka could finish his sentence, I shoved my sickle through his back. He fired his pistol into the ground and managed to take a few steps before he hit the ground, stone dead.

Momma looked at me with such pride in her eyes. From that time on, she knew I had it in me to do what was necessary. She stepped over Joe Bob's body, took my hand and we disappeared into the woods. Joe Bob was the first man I ever killed. Looking back on it now, I have to admit, it felt good.

CHAPTER 3

The Partnership

Mr. Conway, an obese, and elderly man, sat on the porch of his grand plantation house. The legs of his favorite rocking chair were strained, creaking, and near their breaking point, as he rocked back and forth, looking over his sprawling property. Hundreds of slaves toiled in the fields in the brutal Georgia, mid-afternoon sun, chopping sugar cane, bailing hay, and tending to the livestock.

A young slave boy, around ten years of age, wearing a brown tattered shirt and equally tattered pants that were too small for him, ran up the front steps of the plantation house. He stood beside Mr. Conway breathing heavily, trying to catch his breath, "Massa, Massa, looks a yonder!", pointing toward the horizon. Mr. Conway strained forward and squinted his eyes as he watched riders make their way up the red-clay road to the main house.

Eight men rode in Calvary formation, two-by-two, as they approached. The last two riders pulled extra horses behind them, with the bodies of dead men lain over the saddles. There was so much blood leaking from the bodies you could see a thin trail of blood all along the main road. The clear leader of the riders was named Bishop, a tall, skinny, white man, with a long jagged scar from his right temple to his chin. He was the only one that rode a beautiful, midnight black stallion but they all wore long, black dusters.

Mr. Conway tapped the young slave boy on the arm and pointed to the porch floor in front of him. The young slave boy quickly moved and dropped down on all fours so Mr. Conway could put both his feet up on the boy's back. He raised his hand into the air and lifted his pointer finger summoning a female slave who quickly approached and lowered the tray she was carrying in front of him. On the tray was a pitcher of tea and a tall empty glass. He removed the glass from the tray and held it up to cue the slave to fill his glass. Mr. Conway sipped the contents of the glass, then nodded and waved his hand dismissing her. She bowed as she backed away from him, turned and entered the main house.

Missy, one of the slave women who attended Nancy's meeting at the shack the night before, gathered sugar cane in the fields as the men rode past. Fear surged down her spine when she heard the hooves of the rider's horses steadily coming up the road. She turned her head slightly in the direction of the riders, and struggled to keep her composure as she began to nervously gather the sugar cane once again.

Bishop and his men reached the main house and paused directly in front of Mr. Conway. In a low raspy tone, he spoke like a Southern Gentleman, "Good day to you, Sir. Might this be the Conway place?" Mr. Conway raised his hand, and summoned a different slave woman. The slave woman grabbed a large fan with a long wooden handle that was leaning on the wall of the main house. She quickly made her way to Mr. Conway and began to fan him.

Conway answered Bishop's question

smugly. "That it is, Sir. And who, may I ask, might you be?"

"My name is Arthur Bishop, Sir." Mr. Conway rubbed his chin while thinking.

"Bishop. Bishop? Might you be Captain Thomas Bishop's boy, of the Georgia Bishops?" Bishop smirked at Mr. Conway, then answered,

"That is correct, Sir." Mr. Conway slapped his knee with excitement.

"Well I'll be damned, ole Thomas' boy, huh! Boy, me and your daddy raised some cane back in the old days together. Yes indeed. Tell me, how is the old coot?"

Bishop reared back in his saddle uncomfortably. "Well sir, my father is no longer among the living." Mr. Conway shaken by the news responded to Bishop apologetically. "I am truly sorry son, I had no idea. How and when did it happen?"

"It's alright Sir, you had no way of knowing. It happened about nine years ago. There was this darky woman agitatin' our niggras, teaching them how to read and such. My father cornered her one night in the act. She must have gotten the drop on him somehow because when we found him, his head was parted like the Red Sea. Me and the boys have been on her trail ever since, but her trail went cold recently. That is until we came across these poor bastards on your property this morning out by an old rundown shack."

Bishop yelled to his men pulling the horses with the bodies over them, "Show him!" The men pulled the bodies off the horses and the corpses hit the ground with a dull thud. Mr. Conway stood and walked down the steps to look at the bodies. He turned the first corpse over. It was the body of Joe-Bob: his skin pale, his lips blue, and fear frozen on his face. Mr. Conway became furious and turned to Bishop,

"Mr. Bishop, it would appear that we have the same problem!"

"It would appear so, Mr. Conway."

Mr. Conway looked up at Bishop and his men. "You boys get down from them horses. We will get you cleaned up and your horses bedded down for the night. You and I, Mr. Bishop, can try to formulate a plan to eradicate this menace from our midst. Over dinner, how does that sound?" Bishop smiled as he climbed off his horse, "Much obliged, Mr. Conway, that's very kind of you, Sir."

Later that evening Mr. Conway, Bishop, and his men ate in the formal dining room of the main house. A doublewide fireplace warmed the dining room, crackling and sizzling as two thick sections of firewood burned in it. Eight ornate silver candelabras were positioned around the dining room and on the dining table, illuminating the entire room. Missy came out of the kitchen carrying a casserole dish shaking nervously. She placed the dish on the table in front of one of Bishop's men. He looked her lustfully up and down. Missy noticed and lowered her eyes as she walked quickly back into the kitchen.

Bishop stood and raised his glass to toast Mr. Conway. His men stood as well, raising their glasses.

"Here's to Mr. Conway and his generous hospitality! Cheers!"

Mr. Conway raised his glass, "To good hunting, Gentlemen!" They all drank from their glasses. Bishop and his men sat once more and began to eat. "Well, Mr. Bishop, do you find Conway Manor to your liking?"

Bishop picked up his knife and fork and cut the meat on his plate. He looked up and noticed Missy nervously standing in the doorway of the kitchen watching him. Bishop stared at Missy as he placed a piece of meat into his mouth. Missy lowered her eyes to the floor, intentionally avoiding eye contact. Bishop placed his fork and knife onto his plate. He lifted his napkin to wipe his mouth. He smiled, placing his napkin back onto the table, keeping his eyes glued to Missy.

"It almost feels like home but... not quite."

Mr. Conway noticed Bishop staring at Missy, smirked and posed a question, "Perhaps after dinner, you and your men would like some exercise of a different sort?"

"Why, Mr. Conway, I had no idea that you were a mind reader as well as a great host. But I prefer to do business before I do pleasure. Is there perhaps somewhere you and I could talk privately?"

"Why certainly, Son." Mr. Conway and Bishop backed their chairs away from the table. "We can talk in my study." Mr. Conway turned to an elderly, male slave standing along the wall behind him. "Cicero, bring a bottle of my best brandy to the study." Cicero bowed, "Yes, Sir Massa Conway. Right away." Mr. Conway and Bishop left the room.

The study's only light was provided by the fireplace, which had a roaring fire going. Both men walked over to the fireplace and stood. Bishop cautiously began the conversation. "Mr. Conway, I have to ask you a question Sir, but my intent is neither to offend nor provoke." Mr. Conway looked at Bishop intrigued. "Well, go on son, ask me."

Cicero interrupted by walking into the room carrying a silver tray with a large bottle of brandy and two glasses on it. He saw they were agitated and shuffled over to them as quickly as his feeble body would carry him. Bishop removed a glass from the tray while Mr. Conway took the other glass and grabbed the bottle off the tray. Cicero quickly turned and left. The two men placed their glasses on a small table to the right of the large stone hearth. Mr. Conway pulled the cork from the neck of the bottle and poured the brandy into Bishop's glass. He then poured some for himself then placed the bottle on the table. The two men lifted their glasses to one another and took a sip of brandy.

Bishop lowered his glass and breathed deeply, then said bluntly, "What do you know about Black Nancy?" Mr. Conway became apprehensive and stuttered, "I..., I..., know just as much as the next man knows I suppose. Most of it is just nigga rumors and legend, you see." Bishop placed his drink down onto the table. Mr. Conway drank his in one gulp and quickly poured himself another.

"They say that she was some kind of fighter in her younger years, and that she educated herself somehow. Shit! It's just a lot of nigga hogwash, if you ask me."

Bishop smiled slyly as he picked up his glass again. He peered at Mr. Conway over his glass, and then shot the contents down his throat, attempting to read Mr. Conway's body language.

"Mr. Conway, this is not the best way to start a business relationship, with you lyin' to me, or me lyin' to you. So for the sake of honesty, no, for the sake of your own health, what do you know about Black Nancy?"

Mr. Conway gulped his glass of brandy,

placed the glass on the table, walked to the other side of the study, and peered out the window in deep thought. "What do I know about Black Nancy? I know that she is a bloodthirsty, darky demon from hell itself. I also know that she uses the Freedom Station to move between plantations. Every slave within five hundred miles worships and protects her. Every goddamned time I find out her whereabouts, I send my men to eradicate her, but they never come back; like those men you found this morning. All in all, counting the boys you found this morning makes an even 20 of my men this bitch has killed."

Bishop picked the bottle up off of the table and poured himself another drink. He dragged Mr. Conway's glass over and filled it. Bishop placed the bottle back onto the table, picked up both glasses, and walked over to Mr. Conway, handing him his glass. "Here Mr. Conway, you look like you could use another one." Mr. Conway turned and took the glass from his hand. Took a quick swig then cleared his throat, "Thank you, Mr. Bishop. I... how can I put this? I don't want you to catch Black Nancy and I'll tell you why." Mr. Conway gulped the remainder of his brandy and became agitated. "I don't want you to catch her because I want the pleasure of watching that black bitch die in slow, agonizing pain. I, too, have lost someone dear to me. I lost my wife and only son at the hands of that demon. So you see, Mr. Bishop, no one's gonna kill that bitch but me!"

Bishop walked up to Mr. Conway until the two of them were face to face, "I beg to differ, Sir. Black Nancy is mine! My father bought her, raised her, fucked her, and trained her, to be what she is. You have neither the manpower nor the skill to bring ole' Nancy down!" Bishop slowly walked back to the fireplace and placed his arm on the mantle staring into the fire.

He turned toward Mr. Conway and continued.

"My father was one of the founding members of a very private, very exclusive, and some would say an overly decadent social club. Now the men who belonged to this club were some of the wealthiest and influential men in the South. Each of these men had their own special brand of needs--their own desires. They were the gods of that world and owned everything and everyone in it. We all had become addicted to it. All the pleasures that a man could ever want were ours. It was our very own Sodom and Gomorrah.

"But the big draw, were the fights. No holds barred contests that pitted fighting slave against fighting slave. Every plantation in Georgia, including some parts of Carolina, was represented. The men involved would purchase certain slaves, with the sole purpose of fighting them in the pit. These slaves were pampered like prized bulls. They were raised away from the other slaves and fed special food. They would be trained in their various specialties of combat all day, instead of working the fields. From the time they could walk until the time they would die, they were treated special.

"There were a few exceptional fighters, but the best of them, male or female, was Black Nancy. She was never even close to being beaten in four years. No one even came close. No one really knows what made her bite the hand that fed her, but she must have killed a dozen people that night. Unfortunately, my father was one of them. That night was the last time I saw Black Nancy or her daughter. So, you see Mr. Conway, if anybody is gonna kill that bitch, its gonna be me."

Bishop took his last sip of brandy, slammed the glass onto the table, glared at Mr. Conway, then turned and left the room. Mr. Conway, seething from the discussion, finished off his glass and replied to himself, "We'll see about that."

CHAPTER 4

The Dream

Momma and I slept by a babbling brook. The sound of the water was soothing, trickling down the creek over the smooth rocks. Sundown in Georgia is my favorite time of day. It is the time when many different colors can be seen in the sky, just before the sun disappears beyond the horizon.

To pass the time I count all the colors of the sky at, what Momma and I like to call, the magic hour. Our camp is a modest one, just a couple of mother nature's own Georgia pine branch beds; which means we place pine branch limbs on the ground, one on top of the other. Momma says the branches stop us from losing body heat through the ground. I just like the piney smell of the branches, it reminds me of Christmas. I could do without all of the sticky sap though.

Every year, back on the plantation, I would sneak over to the big house and peek through the window to watch the Bishop's decorate their Christmas tree. I'd close my eyes and wish as hard as I could that one day momma and I would have our very own Christmas tree in our very own house. But momma says that Christmas was not for us black folk. It was only for the white man.

Tonight I volunteered to take the first watch because momma seems to be more tired than usual. She hardly sleeps a wink anymore, which worries me deeply. Momma began to toss and turn in her sleep again last night. She's been prone to having violent nightmares for as long as I can remember. I had to shake her three times last night before she woke up panting and sweating. What scared me the most, she appeared not to know where she was.

"Momma, are you alright?" I whispered nervously. She just nodded with the strangest expression on her face. "I made you the very last of the coffee. I hope you like it", trying to get her to talk. When I pulled the tin from the fire, I had to use the bottom of my dress because the contents were steaming with heat. Momma had to use the bottom of her dress too. She looked into the can and swirled the contents around. She took a small sip and immediately spit the black liquid out of her mouth, splashing it onto the pine branches.

It happened so suddenly I had to choke back my laughter. That irritated momma and she scowled, "Little girl, are you tryin' to poison me?" She threw the can on the ground and spit continuously to remove the gritty taste from her mouth. Still giggling, I covered my mouth with my hand and let her know why the last of the coffee was horrid. "Oh yeah, we ran out of sugar." Momma smiled replying, "You don't say." We both looked at each other and fell out laughing. I love laughing with Momma because it so rarely happens and it's usually short lived.

Momma went over to the creek and knelt on the bank to wash in its cool waters. I followed. Still curious about her nightmare I asked, "What was the nightmare about this time? You scare me when you're screaming and fighting in your sleep." She stopped bathing and stared blankly at the flowing creek.

"I dreamt I was still on the Bishop Plantation. Captain Bishop was sneaking out of his wife's bed. He quietly made his way down the steps of the main house, and came to the barn, where they kept us fighters. He looked into the first stall, where Billy was all skin and bones because Captain Bishop wanted to see how long an African boy could last without food.

"The Captain walked by the next stall and looked in. He saw another one of the boys, chained up like an animal, in the stall. The boy, terrified, cringed in the darkness like trapped prey.

"Finally, the Captain got to mine. I wanted to scream but when I opened my mouth no sound came out. He began to give me what he called his 'special touch' and I could not move."

At that moment I couldn't believe what I was seeing-- a tear rolled down momma's cheek. It was the first time I had ever seen my momma cry. I hurried over and brushed her hair with my hand with as much love as I could summon. She regained her composure and stood abruptly saying, "Time to move."

CHAPTER 5

Thou Shalt Not Kill

While walking through the woods that day I began to feel the guilt of having killed another human being the night before. All I could see was my sickle plunging deep into that man's back. I also remembered how my sickle felt as it slid into him, severing organs, puncturing muscle and scraping against bone. Inside of my head passages from momma's bible of the Ten Commandments THOU SHALT NOT KILL echoed. My palms were clammy and the fear of hellfire danced in my mind. Confusion grew with each step. Momma as usual, kept her eyes and ears trained on every movement and sound in the forest.

I decided, after miles of walking, just to ask her... "Momma, are we going to hell?" She looked back at me quizzically, "Child, now where on earth did you get a notion like that into your head?"

"From the bible, momma. It says in the bible, 'Thou shall not kill'." She sighed and said, "I think you misunderstood that passage, baby. What it really says is, 'thou shall not try to kill momma, and momma will not try to kill you.' "

I stopped walking. Momma kept on until she realized I wasn't. She turned and walked back to me. "Ruby, what's wrong with you? We gotta keep moving." That's when I broke down, "Momma, I still see the man I killed when I close my eyes. It gives me a sick feeling inside." I began to cry. Momma came to me and hugged me tightly. "Don't you shed one tear for them peckawoods or any other person who enslaves and rapes you and yours.

"You have to understand this Ruby, all I have is you and all you have is me in this shitty world. I know all of this is hard to understand, but we have to try to educate as many of our people as we can..."

I became angry with her and blurted out, "How can you and me change anything, momma?! We're just two black woman in the middle of a sea of white!"

Momma stopped hugging me and bent at the waist until she and I were face-to-face. Sternly she rebutted, "We are not just two black women, like you say. We are two strong African women in a sea of white. Remember this always baby, a flood starts with only two tiny drops of rain. Well girl, we are those drops of rain and I plan to rain on every cracka who put his dirty hands on my baby and treats our people no better than livestock!"

Momma turned and began to walk away. Following closely behind her I asked another question, "Why do you have to risk our lives trying to teach a slave how to read?" She stopped abruptly once more and turned back towards me scowling, "For the same reason they don't want them to, baby. For the same reason they don't want them to!" She turned and continued walking through the woods. I pondered her words for the remainder of the day, finally gleaning the meaning of them by nightfall. Relieved.

CHAPTER 6

Abbey Copper

Momma and I arose just before dawn to strike camp. We trudged through dense forest for hours, until coming upon a small clearing in the center of these thick, foliated woods. A small blue house sat in the middle of the clearing. Thick, white smoke bellowed from the chimney. White, painted, ornate shutters hung on the windows. It was a curious house in a more curious place. Just as I was imagining what type of people lived there, the front door of the house swung open, as if someone was watching us. So we took cover and dashed behind a large pine tree.

A portly, white woman stepped out of the house whistling a cheerful tune. She walked around to the side of the house where a sizable woodpile lay. She grabbed a section of log off the pile and placed it onto the chopping block. She grabbed the axe that was leaning against the chopping block, and began to chop firewood.

We carefully made our way up to the house. Momma slowly peeked around the corner to watch the woman. She reached over her shoulder, and pulled one of the sickles from behind her head, slowly as to not make a sound. She turned placing her pointer finger to her mouth, signaling me to be quiet. Momma stepped around the corner of the house and crept up on the unsuspecting woman. Once momma was in striking distance, she raised her sickle into the air, preparing to strike.

The woman placed another log onto the block seemingly unaware of momma's presence. She raised the axe over her head, and swung it, not at the log, but around at momma. Momma blocked the axe skillfully with her sickle. The two tools clanked together loudly and created sparks when they collided. I was scared and shocked at the same time; never had I seen anyone block one of momma's strikes so easily.

Both of their weapons were locked together. They were face-to-face and eye-to-eye, both of them straining and gritting their teeth. I was on edge until, thankfully, I saw the woman break into a smile, then momma as well. The woman dropped her axe to the ground and momma returned her sickle to its harness on her back. Momma laughed. Then yelled, "I could've had you, old woman!"

"Humph, that'll be the day! Hell, I smelled you two a mile off!"

"I could've had you, you old, white, woman you!" Momma scoffed playfully.

"You wouldn't do that to ole' Abbey Copper, would ya?"

"And why the hell not?"

"Cause', I'm the only friend your runaway ass has got"! Abbey teased. Momma said, "You know what woman?"

"What?" Abbey replied.

"You're right!" The two of them laughed hysterically and hugged each other tightly, like two sisters seeing each other for the first time in years.

It appeared to be safe enough to make my presence known, so I walked from behind the house to where momma and Abbey were talking.

When Miss Abbey saw me she was very surprised at how much I had grown.

"Oh my God, is that... is that Ruby?! My, you've grown into quite the little woman, haven't you? You two come on into the house. I'll get you washed up and get some vittles into ya!" She picked up a few cut pieces of firewood, and we followed her into the house.

CHAPTER 7

I Want The Names

The morning after the heated discussion in Mr. Conway's study, all of the slaves on the plantation were summoned and instructed to report to the main house immediately. Per his custom, Mr. Conway rocked back and forth on the big porch, in his favorite rickety rocking chair. The field hands gathered in the front courtyard, directly in front of he and Bishop. Bishop stood on the ground watching the field hands dubiously, as he rubbed the scarlet colored scar on his face.

Not knowing why they had been summoned, the slaves cowered nervously, as they stood in front of Mr. Conway and Bishop. Bishop's men took positions around the gathered slaves, muskets and pistols at the ready.

Mr. Conway stopped rocking in his chair,

stood, and walked to the white, painted railing that surrounded the porch. He looked over his gathered slaves, scowling. He took a deep breath and pointed toward Bishop.

"This man is Mr. Bishop. He has come here to Conway Manor looking for the fugitive slave called Black Nancy. I am also interested in finding this woman. Last night some of you standing here went out to meet with this criminal, and many of my men are dead, by her hand!"

Missy lowered her head fearing that these men already knew she attended the clandestine meeting the night before. Her body trembled uncontrollably and she found it nearly impossible to contain her fear. Her hands began to shake, her breathing labored. She locked her fingers together in an attempt to stop them from shaking. She felt at any minute the men would identify her and do horrible things to her.

Mr. Conway continued, "I want the names of all of the filth who went up to the old shack last night, or just step forward. If you step forward now, the punishment won't be as severe as if you do not!" Mr. Conway placed his hands behind his back like a dignitary. The slaves began to murmur and look around at one another. Missy knew, all too well, what the penalty was for consorting with Black Nancy.

Missy turned and gave the three other women that came with her to the shack the night before, a look of desperation; as if she was going to burst into flames at any second. The youngest of the women, Daisy, realized Missy was thinking of giving herself up. She carefully shook her head NO toward Missy, but Missy ignored the girl's warning. She turned back and faced Bishop and Mr. Conway.

Mr. Conway became more agitated with each passing moment. None of the slaves stepped forward. He screamed at them. "Now you niggers better come forward, or there will be hell to pay on your children!"

Each slave mother clutched her child. The slaves began to murmur once again amongst each other. Missy not wanting anyone else to suffer for something she had done, closed her eyes and summoned all of her courage. She slowly opened them, looked to the sky and said a silent prayer as she placed her right bare foot forward. The murmuring turned to dead silence immediately, when the other slaves saw Missy step forward. Missy shook uncontrollably, as she uttered the nearly inaudible words, "I... it was me, Massa Conway, Sir. I be the one that you and dat' there man, is lookin' for." The three girls who were with her the night before, cringed. Tears filled their eyes as they watched Missy commit her selfless act.

Bishop walked over to Missy, slowly looking her up and down in disgust as he did so. Mr. Conway scanned the rest of the slaves looking for the slightest hint of guilt on any of their faces or body language. Like a scolding parent, he yelled at Missy, "Who else was wit ya girl? Don't you dare lie to me!" Missy lifted her head up to Mr. Conway, "I would never lie to you, Massa. I be the only one that went out there to see Nancy last night. I swears!"

Bishop stood in front of Missy, glaring at her and studying her every move, as lies fell from her quivering lips. He turned toward Mr. Conway and sneered, "This black bitch is lyin!" "How can you be so sure?" Mr. Conway asked. Bishop removed a pair of thick leather riding gloves from the waist of his pants. He stared at Missy as he slowly pulled the gloves onto his hands. He answered Mr. Conway's query, with his eyes trained on her, "Because, when we found those bodies out by the shack, one of the bodies was that of a dead nigger, with his face bashed in."

Mr. Conway turned and walked down the steps of the porch to ground level. Once there, he quickly walked over to Missy and slapped her to the ground. The other slaves backed away from Mr. Conway and Missy. She cried out for help and attempted to crawl away on all fours. But Mr. Conway ran up beside her and with all of his strength and kicked her in the stomach. She screamed in piercing pain, as she was flipped to her back from the force of the blow. Mr. Conway was in a crazed state and looked like a mad man. He was lathered in sweat and squinting from the morning sun, yelled, "The rest of you niggers get out of my fucking sight, before I kill the lot of you!" Then without any thought, turned and began to stomp and kick Missy once again.

Bishop and his men stood and watched

the savage beating of Missy. They seemed to be getting pleasure with each moan Missy made, until all of them were all smiles and encircling Mr. Conway and Missy, as if they were at a pit fight. Mr. Conway continued kicking her until he became too winded. But not before her left eye was closed and grotesquely swollen, her nose was broken and she coughed up blood.

Bishop coolly strolled over to Mr. Conway. "Mr. Conway, are you done, by any chance?" Still attempting to catch his breath, Mr. Conway stood up straight and turned to Bishop, "Yeah I'm done. What do want to do with her?" Bishop smirked then walked over to Missy and grabbed her by the back collar of her dress. He started toward the back of the property to the barn, dragging her through the dirt. Missy desperately begged, "No, Please no! No! No! No..."

Bishop yelled back to Mr. Conway, "This girl is the last thing around here still alive, to see ole Nancy. I need to know which way she was headed. And I guarantee that this little lady is gonna tell me everything I need to know!" One of his men held the barn door open as he dragged

Missy into the darkness of the barn. Once inside, the door was slammed behind him.

Daisy, the youngest of the three slave girls who went to the shack, scowled as she watched Bishop disappear into the barn with Missy. Her two sisters huddled together, sobbing. She looked up at them angrily and spat, "Dem peckawoods ain't gotta treat Missy that way. I hope one day, dem crackas do run into Nancy and her sickles! Then they heathen heads gonna roll!" Daisy's older sister Karen looked down at her and chides, "Girl, you betta hush yo' mouth before one of them crackas' hears you." Daisy stared at the barn and yelled defiantly, "I don't care if they hear me!"

Karen walked up behind Daisy and grabbed her, trying to calm her down but their other sister, Charlotte, was surprisingly unaffected and dismissive. Karen tried again to reason with her baby sister. "Daisy, I don't know what has gotten into you, but you need to calm yourself down, or all of us gonna' be in that barn. Not just Missy." She blessed herself, making the sign of cross, as she looked at the barn and shook her head.

Charlotte sighed nonchalantly and spoke to Daisy as well. "Now Daisy," in her high pitched voice, "Missy knew what she was doin'. She knew what could happen if we was caught." Karen and Daisy looked at Charlotte ashamed. Karen sneered, "Charlotte, Missy is in that barn yonder, because she knew if she didn't take the blame, all of us would of been in there. It was a very brave thing she did, and we should never forget it."

Charlotte acted indifferently and unmoved by Karen's rebuttal. "Hell, it was her idea to go out there to meet miss high and mighty Nancy anyway. Everybody thinks that nigga walks on water or somethin'. Humph, if you ask me, it only be a matter of time till them crackas haul her black ass up in there too!"

Daisy suddenly ran toward her bigger sister and dove into her. They tumbled onto the ground, rolling through the dirt and grass. Although Charlotte out weighed Daisy by at least 80 pounds, little ole' Daisy gave her all she could handle. Karen struggled to break the two away from each other. Once separated, they jumped to their feet; still breathing heavily, completely covered in red dust. Charlotte scowled at Daisy, while brushing the dust off her clothes, "You two can do whatever the hell you want, but I'm done with this mess!" She stomped away from both of them.

Still wanting to get at her older sister, Daisy continued to struggle in the strong, steady arms of Karen, who struggled to hold Daisy at bay while Charlotte left the area. Once Charlotte was a safe enough distance away, Karen, in her most calm and soothing voice, whispered into Daisy's ear, "Shhhh, calm down little sister. Calm down." Daisy finally responded to her sister's wishes and began to calm herself and regain her composure. She turned her head towards Karen, and with tears in her eyes, cried, "I just can't believe that my own flesh and blood does not see how much our people need Miss Nancy. Well, you know what? I sure as hell ain't gonna sit around this place and do nothing!"

Karen looked at her sister with concern. "Daisy, really, what can you do?" Daisy brushed the grass and dust from her hair, and looked directly into Karen's eyes with fearless determination and snapped, "I can warn Miss

Nancy about this new white man that's huntin' her. That's what I can do!"

Karen thought to herself for a moment, then spoke sternly but concerned. "Alright! But you have to promise me you'll be careful little girl." Daisy finally broke into a smile and hugged Karen tightly. "I'll be careful, I promise. I'll leave tonight, when everything goes dark in the big house." Karen nodded to Daisy and held her tightly with both arms, as if she was going off to war.

Late that same evening, the sisters lay on the dirt floor of their slave hut. Daisy pretended to be asleep. She rolled over quietly, noticing Karen was not sleeping, but sitting up staring at her. Daisy heard Charlotte breathing heavy, a sure sign she was sleeping soundly. Karen smiled at Daisy and mouthed the words "BE-CARE-FUL" to her. Daisy responded in the same fashion, "I-WILL."

She stood silently and walked toward the door of the hut. She placed a black shawl hanging by the door over her head and face. She opened the door of the hut slowly, as not to make a sound. Halfway open the door creaked loudly. She paused and threw a look at Charlotte, who still appeared to be sleeping soundly. Daisy released the breath she was holding, opened the door and left.

Karen made the sign of the cross, and said a quiet prayer. She closed her eyes and lay down on her blanket. Charlotte, only pretending to be asleep, opened her eyes and jumped to her feet. She looked down at Karen and furiously said, "Where the hell do she think she goin'?" Karen sat up angrily and retorted, "She goin' to warn Nancy about them new crackas." Charlotte threw a fit: "Have you lost your goddamned mind? Lettin' that child go warn the most wanted nigger in all the land? Do you have any idea how many crackas are lookin' for Nancy? Shit! That was just dumb! If somethin' happens to that girl, it'll be your fault!"

Outside, Daisy quietly made her way past the main house. The only light was that of the full moon hanging low in the night sky. She sprinted as fast as she could across the yard, past the main house, to the barn. She could see light coming from the torches held by Bishop's men, as it shone through the cracks in the wallboards of the barn.

Daisy heard Missy's screams of agony coming from inside. She hid behind the barn and peeked inside through one of the cracks in the wall. She bit her lip and cringed when she saw the horrible condition of her friend Missy. Bishop and his men had Missy hanging by her feet, from the rafters, naked with multiple severe burns on her body and legs. Her hands were tied tightly together behind her back with barbed wire. A few feet away from where she hung, was a fire with three different branding irons lying in the amber coals.

Bishop walked over to the fire and placed the branding iron he was holding, into its infernal heat. He grabbed one of the other branding irons from the fire. Its tip glowed red hot like the color of lava. He slowly approached Missy with the branding iron. "Now you're gonna tell me where Nancy was headed, ain't you?" Missy, trembled, whimpered, her voice barely audible, "I ain't telling you shit, Cracka..." and spat blood at him.

Bishop lost his temper, and placed the red-hot branding iron onto Missy's side. Steam bellowed from the hot metal scorching her flesh. The smell of burning meat filled the air. Missy screamed in agony once more and wriggled like a fish caught on the line, making the ropes dig deeper into her bloody ankles.

Daisy covered her mouth, attempting to keep down her food. The smell of Missy's burning flesh was awful. Unable to watch anymore she turned away from the barn and ran as fast as she could into the woods on her way to find Nancy.

Bishop took the branding iron and placed it back into the fire. He walked back over to Missy, "You gonna tell me what I want to know, bitch, or I'm gonna burn the rest of your hide clean off. Do you understand me?" He walked to the fire and pulled another branding iron from it with a longer heated surface than the prior one. He turned and walked slowly toward Missy. She wriggled and whimpered in fear as Bishop approached her once more. He knelt down to the level where they were face-to-face. He slowly raised the branding iron near Missy's face. The branding iron was so hot it illuminated her cheek. Bishop spat on the iron. It sizzled like butter on a hot skillet. He looked into Missy's face and smiled sinisterly, "Oh, you gonna tell me something, gal."

He began to place the branding iron onto Missy's face when he was abruptly interrupted by one of his men entering the barn. His man walked over to him and whispered into his ear. Bishop turned toward Missy and smirked. He walked slowly toward her once more with the branding iron in his right hand. She squirmed in anticipation of the searing heat of the iron cooking into her already blistered flesh. Bishop instead walked passed her this time to the fire and placed the iron back into it. He smirked as he walked past a still trembling and horrified Missy and left the barn with her still dangling from the rafters.

CHAPTER 8

What's A Street?

Oh my God! Now I know why white folks are always making such a big deal about getting into a hot tub of water. This is the life! I'm in Miss Abbey's large metal tub, complete with water that could burn the fur off a jackrabbit, but it feels so good. Momma's washing my hair and humming her favorite spiritual, *Peace, Be Still*. It's been a long time since momma and I have had the chance to relax a bit and be just mother and daughter-- not hounded fugitives.

Miss Abbey just came in with another steaming bucket of hot water for the tub. She poured it into my bath and I jumped up to complain but, before I could utter my protest, Miss Abbey said, "Quit your fussin'! Is it because the water is hot, or is it the dirt you're covered in is mad that you're washing it off?" She laughed hysterically and left the room. I made a funny face at her and stuck my tongue out as she left, taking care she didn't see me.

I figured I was done, but momma grabbed my hips and forced me back down into the water. She began to wash my hair again. All of a sudden, a nagging question came into my mind. I hesitated for a moment, because the subject I was about to broach had been a very touchy one in the past, but one I had to ask anyway, "Momma?"

"Yes, baby", she said softly, while wringing my hair out.

"Do you think we could live in a nice house like Miss Abbey's one day?"

"I don't see why not. I've heard tales of some cities up North where black folks live on the same street as white folks."

"You mean, on the same street!" I squealed with excitement.

"Yes, on the same street."

I closed my eyes and tried to imagine what it would be like living on the same street as white folks. The notion seemed unbelievable, but then, I realized something, "Momma?"

"Yes, baby?"

"What's a street?"

I had no idea what a street was. Momma paused and looked down at me. We burst into uncontrollable laughter. Momma gave my hair a few more squeezes with her strong hands and dunked my lathered head under the bath water to rinse. She stood over me, with her hands on her hips, smiling proudly, "Come on out of there and dry off. It's my turn to get clean."

I grabbed the towel hanging on the rim of the tub and wrapped it around myself. I thanked momma for washing my hair, put my dress back on and started downstairs.

Miss Abbey looked so calm, rocking in her rocking chair by a roaring fire in the fireplace. She was so focused on reading from a large bible on her lap that I don't think she even noticed my nosey-self walking around her house. I rubbed my head with the towel to dry it and continued my tour around Miss Abbey's house, looking at pictures and knickknacks she had sitting on shelves all through her quaint little house. I came across a three-portrait, brass picture frame, on a shelf by itself. One photo was of a white man with a long beard, and the other of a thin, freckled-faced boy, no older than me. The last photo was of a much younger, slimmer Miss Abbey. I yelled, "Miss Abbey, is this your husband and son?" Miss Abbey stopped reading and peeked at me over her glasses. "Yes, that's my husband Charles, and the little boy, that's my Samuel."

I removed the picture frame from the shelf and studied them further. "So where are they now, Miss Abbey?" Miss Abbey closed the bible and placed it onto a small wooden table next to her rocking chair. She got up and slowly walked over toward me, kind of sad. Not saying a word, she took the pictures from me and looked lovingly at them. A crooked smile broke on her face as she stood their reminiscing.

"So, where are they now, Miss Abbey"? I asked again. She suddenly became very sad. "My son, Samuel, was taken by consumption a few years back. My husband Charles wasn't that lucky. They found out that he helped a black family escape up North, so to teach us a lesson, he was strung up by lowdown, dirty, Georgia, white trash."

I felt like such an idiot for even asking her. To say I was uncomfortable would be a gross understatement.

"I'm terribly sorry, Miss Abbey, I didn't mean to pry."

She forced another smile. "I know, Baby. It's alright. People always say that out in these woods is no place for a widowed woman to be living alone. But, you know what I say to those people?" Miss Abbey placed the pictures back onto the shelf gently and turned to me.

"What's that?", I asked.

"Get out of my fuckin' house, and mind your own goddamned business!"

I jumped back, startled and tickled at Miss Abbey's spunky response. I could see why she and momma were such good friends. She stared at the two photos for a moment and I could see tears well up in the corners of her eyes. She returned to her seat by the fireplace and looked into the fire again, reminiscing about the family she once had.

Still staring deep into the fire, she continued, "But, in all truthfulness, my husband is the very reason why I stay here. My Charles saw this house as a weigh station between heaven and hell. It is a safe haven for those who would not live in bondage anymore. He would say with full conviction, *'Some things in this world are just worth dying for.'* That's the reason this place is used as a Freedom Station and will be, till my dying day."

I stood there watching this old white woman talking about risking her life, and her husband giving his life for my people. This notion confused me, as I had heard tale of some whites up North making a little fuss over the abolishment of slavery, but I never thought I would meet one, in a thicket, in the middle of Georgia no less.

Our short conversation definitely endeared Miss Abbey to me. She began to rock in her rocker once more when momma entered the living room. "What are you two up to down here?" Momma said, as she rubbed a towel on her head to dry it. Miss Abbey quickly answered, "Oh, I was just telling your daughter some of my old war stories." Miss Abbey stood and pointed to the chair she had vacated and offered it to momma.

"Here Nancy, come dry your hair by the fire."

"Thank you." Momma smiled and took a seat.

CHAPTER 9

Charlotte's Web

Mr. Conway was sitting by the fireplace sipping a glass of brandy. He wept as he sat staring at a small golden picture frame. Suddenly there was a knock at the door. Cicero, his elderly male house slave, opened the door to the study and entered. "Cuse me, Massa Conway, Sir" he said.

Mr. Conway quickly wiped his eyes and stood attempting to conceal his sadness. "Yes, what do you want?" he barked. Cicero lowered his head and replied in a subtle, even tone, "Sir, Mr. Bishop is here to see you." Mr. Conway placed the picture frame back onto the mantle over the fireplace and turned toward the door.

"Well, show the man in, Cicero!"

"Yes'em. Massa, Sir!" Cicero turned and left the study.

Bishop entered the study a few moments later with a devilish grin on his face.

"How are you, Mr. Conway? Please excuse me for disturbing you at such an hour."

Mr. Conway sat in his chair by the fireplace once more. He looked up at Bishop quizzically, "Is this about that slave girl you've been torturing all blasted day? What? Did she talk?" Bishop sighed and looked down at the floor.

"No Sir, she didn't. But, we did receive an early Christmas gift this year." Becoming more puzzled than before, Mr. Conway frowned,

"Gift? What kind of gift?"

He was visibly disturbed and annoyed with Bishop's toying around.

Bishop lifted his head coyly and slowly walked toward the door of the study. He opened it. Charlotte was standing on the other side of the door smiling from ear to ear. Still confused about Bishop's intentions, Mr. Conway pointed toward Charlotte angrily, "This bed wench is the gift?"

Charlotte, seizing the opportunity, sashayed over to Mr. Conway and eased onto his lap. She placed her arms around the back of his neck and looked deeply into his eyes. In a sultry tone, beguiled him, "Yes Sir, mass' Conway, I be your gift. You see ole Charlotte know exactly where Black Nancy be headed."

Mr. Conway became extremely agitated and jumped up from his chair, throwing a startled Charlotte to the floor. She crawled away from him afraid, pausing only after reaching where Bishop was standing. She stood, taking refuge behind a smirking Bishop. Mr. Conway still aggravated at the situation, pointed at Charlotte, "You little black bitch! You tell me where Black Nancy is or I'll whip every bit of black off your godforsaken hide!"

Bishop lifted his right hand slightly, to calm Mr. Conway down. Calmly he said, "Mr. Conway, I understand that you're upset, but no more so than I. Now, little Miss Charlotte has come forth, to volunteer the information that you and I are in dire need of. Surely, that has to count for something."

Mr. Conway pondered Bishop's words. He began to regain his composure. Charlotte peeked around Bishop's back like a scared child. Bishop continued to smirk at Mr. Conway while waiting for his reply. Finally, Mr. Conway was calm enough to reply. He walked slowly toward Bishop and Charlotte, "So, what do you want child?"

Charlotte slowly stepped from behind Bishop. She twirled the bottom of her dress around the pointer finger on her right hand like a child about to ask for an expensive Christmas gift.

"All I wants, Sir, is better food for me and my sisters. Oh, and less work in the fields and on occasion..." she blushed, then smiled, "I want to come and keep you warm on some a 'dem cold nights, Sir. Oh, and there is one other thing..."

Mr. Conway became inpatient with her. "What is that, little girl? My patience is wearing thin!"

"I don't want anything to happen to my little sister", she said nervously. Mr. Conway, wrinkling his forehead asked, "Daisy? What does Daisy have to do with any of this?"

Bishop walked over to the table, and poured himself a drink. "Apparently, Daisy ran off earlier this evening to warn Black Nancy about me and my men. She has a pretty good head start too." Mr. Conway looked at Bishop wondering why he was taking this news of Daisy so well.

"You don't seem to be in a hurry to catch Black Nancy before that girl warns her", said Mr. Conway. Bishop replied smugly, "Mr. Conway, I have a man following her right this very moment." Mr. Conway looked at Bishop confused. "If you already had a man following the girl to where Black Nancy is, why in the hell would you bring this black trollop into my home?" Bishop looked down at Charlotte and smugly answered, "Because she's your property and I wanted to see her face when I told you that I had a man following her sister already."

At that moment, a chill ran down Charlotte's spine. Her stomach muscles tightened as she realized that Bishop was toying with her. The horrible realization hit her like a brick in the face -- him having a man already following her sister meant he did not really need her in the first place. She began to back away from Bishop toward the door of the study. Bishop and Mr. Conway slowly turned towards her. Bishop's tone turned sinister. "Mr. Conway,

Sir, what kind of guest would I be, if I didn't ask if I could do whatever I wanted to this here little lying, conniving Philly?"

Mr. Conway laughed hysterically at Charlotte, slapping his knee. Bishop looked on as he took a shot of brandy, then joined in on the laughter. Charlotte, dejected and ashamed, turned and opened the study door quickly to escape. Much to her dismay, one of Bishop's men was waiting for her on the other side of the door. He cocked his pistol and pointed it at Charlotte's forehead. She froze in fear as urine began to trickle down her legs, forming a small puddle on the floor.

Mr. Conway smiled, shook his head in playful disbelief at the strategic prowess of Bishop. "Mr. Bishop, I like your style, Sir. You and your men can have that girl, with my compliments!" Bishop nodded in appreciation towards Mr. Conway and asked, "After we're done, shall we bring her back?" Mr. Conway walked over to the table, and poured himself another glass of brandy. He drank while turning his back to Bishop and Charlotte, then answered with finality, "Don't bother." and slammed the empty glass onto the table.

Charlotte realizing her fate, cringed and crumbled to the floor in a ball, sobbing. Bishop tipped his hat to Mr. Conway. He turned to his man standing over Charlotte and nodded. The man picked Charlotte up off the floor and slung her over his shoulder like a sack of potatoes. Bishop smirked as he began to slowly close the door of the study.

Mr. Conway thought to himself, then, suddenly called out, "Mr. Bishop!" Bishop stopped closing the door and peeked back into the study. "Yes, Sir?" With a determined and focused expression on his face, Mr. Conway spoke. "You and your men have all the fun you can tonight. For tomorrow we hunt!" Bishop smiled widely, then confidently answered, "That we do, Sir. That we do." Bishop closed the door.

Outside of the study, Bishop glared at a sobbing Charlotte with disgust. "You thought you were so fucking smart, didn't you, nigger? Well, you're mine now, gal. Time to show you how we play with little hot-in-the-ass nigga gals down Carolina way." He grinned sinisterly at his man holding the pistol to Charlotte's head. His man grabbed a hand full of her hair and placed his pistol back into its holster. He dragged Charlotte kicking and screaming by the hair down the hall, then down the winding wooden staircase of the main house

The house slaves watched in terror as Bishop walked down the stairs proudly in front of his man and Charlotte, who was grasping desperately for the railing. Bishop's man tugged at her a few times trying to dislodge her hands from the railing. Finally growing inpatient, he removed his pistol from its holster and slammed it butt side first onto Charlotte's tightly clasped hands. Charlotte shrieked as he smashed her fingers with his pistol butt.

She released the railing, then was dragged down the remaining stairs. Grinding her fingernails to nubs, she tried to claw the floorboards to keep from being taken, but to no avail. Bishop, once at the huge white front door, tipped his hat to Cicero mockingly, as they dragged Charlotte out of the house.

Cicero shook his head in despair for Charlotte and closed the door behind them. He walked into the kitchen where all of the house slaves had congregated. They all looked at one another somberly. Cicero walked to the middle of the kitchen and hung his head. Everyone else in the kitchen walked over to him and joined hands forming a prayer circle. They all bowed their heads, closed their eyes and collectively prayed in silence for Charlotte. Her muffled screams could be heard across the whole of the plantation as Bishop and his men began to rape and torture her. Agonizing screams and drunken laughter filled the air all night.

At first light the following morning, Bishop and his men sat atop their horses awaiting the arrival of Mr. Conway. A young slave boy held the reins of a beautiful brown stallion. Mr. Conway came out of the house wearing full riding regalia. He walked down the steps of the main house and mounted the stallion held by the slave boy. Placing his feet into the stirrups with the assistance of the boy, he turned to Bishop excitedly, "A beautiful day to hunt, wouldn't you say, Mr. Bishop?" Bishop replied coldly, "Sir, everyday is a good day to hunt black bitches."

Bishop tipped his hat to a smiling Mr.

Conway, then, gave his men a hand gesture signaling them to move out. Mr. Conway rode up to Bishop, leaned over and said, "We'll meet up with the rest of my boys by the creek on the way. I instructed them to bring the hounds." Bishop nodded to him in approval, then they all rode away from the main house.

Mr. Conway spat a large wad of phlegm on the ground, disrespectfully, in the direction of the lifeless bodies of Missy and Charlotte, which hung upside down from a large branch of an ancient oak tree on the property. Their bodies swayed from side to side in the morning breeze gently like Spanish moss. Both their bodies were badly beaten and covered with blisters. Charlotte's eyes were closed as if she was only sleeping, but Missy's eyes were open, with the horror and anguish of the night's ordeal frozen upon her face.

CHAPTER 10

Practice

I cannot remember sleeping so comfortably in my entire life. When I awoke this morning, the sun was shining through the window and I could feel its warmth on my face. I remember thinking to myself the saying "feels like home", must mean this. Last night was my first time ever sleeping on a feather-stuffed mattress. Now, I understood why white folks make such a fuss about them.

When I opened my eyes, I could also feel momma's glare upon me, which could only mean one thing...sickle practice! I rolled over, and sure enough, momma was in full fight kit, standing over me. "Practice time, Missy! Get your lazy butt from under those sheets and meet me out back!" she ordered. I gave her my traditional response of sighing and moaning, trying to dissuade her from wanting to practice.

As usual, she ignored me, and walked out of the room, sickles in hand. Much to my displeasure, I gave up my cozy snug-as-a-bug feeling under those warm, lilac smelling sheets, and grabbed my gear to join momma out back of Miss Abbey's house. It was right then and there I planned to show momma the level of my fighting skills. I thought, hell, I know some shit too. She has only been teaching me how to fight for the past nine years. Some of it was bound to rub off.

When I exited the house, momma was standing in her ready position. She stood on the opposite side of Miss Abbey's yard, studying my every stride until I got into my ready position. Her now infamous, or famous sickles, depending upon which race of people you asked, grasped tightly in each of her hands. Her breathing intentionally slowed and focused. Finally reaching a spot in the yard I could start from, I stopped and turned sharply towards her, clutching my sickles tightly in my hands as well. Momma smirked, then yelled across the yard, "Whenever you're ready, Baby!"

I smiled briefly, and channeled my inner warrior-- slowing my breathing. I attempted to focus my thoughts as momma had taught me. I closed my eyes briefly and reopened them quickly. Without warning, I started my war cry, as I tried to surprise momma by charging her immediately. Momma smirked as she waited for my impromptu sneak attack.

Once close enough to strike, I swung my sickles rapidly, first the right, then the left. Momma, without any strain whatsoever, calmly blocked every one of my attempted strikes at her; the metal from our sickles meeting made loud clanking noises and made many sparks fly.

The first stage of my attack was concentrated above her waist with no success. I decided to attack her lower, by swinging my right sickle at her legs. She jumped with the agility of a deer over my attempted blow and went on the offensive. Momma began to attack me with her sickles. No matter how many times she and I practiced together, I still marveled at how strong and skillful she was. She struck with such blinding speed and precision it caused me to back away from her as I struggled to block them.

I finally found myself with nowhere to run. Before I knew it, I had backed myself up to the wall of the house. Momma raised the sickle in her right hand above her head about to deal the final blow. I could see the veins popping in her forehead and her teethed clenched--these are the times I pray to God, that she realizes I'm her baby girl. But slowly a smile crept onto her smoothed-skin face. We both laughed hardily while breathing heavily from all of the physical exertion.

Momma lowered her arm and walked to the rain barrel filled with water next to the house. She turned to me still winded, "You are still keeping your left guard much too low!" Still attempting to catch my breath, I walked over to the barrel as well. "Huh! That's what you say. I'm just makin' up my own style is all, momma!" Momma threw her sickles into the ground, sticking the tips only, keeping the handles at a height they could be grabbed again quickly. She cupped her hands and scooped water to drink from the barrel. Trying to impress her, I threw my sickles to the ground in a similar fashion trying to stick the tips into the ground as she did. But, my sickles slowly leaned then fell to the ground.

A little embarrassed, I decided to place my entire face into the barrel of cool water. When I lifted my head out of the barrel, momma was looking at me with a disappointed look on her face. She placed her hand back into the barrel and rubbed some water on her neck. "You need to take this more seriously. Proper technique will save your life one day, little girl. I won't be around forever, you know." she said, in her most condescending, motherly tone.

I placed my head into the barrel again, trying to drown momma's lecture out. She became annoyed, "Do you hear what I'm telling you!" I knew she would not leave it alone, so I answered, "Yes momma, I hear you." Momma knew the subject of her not being here one day, was a topic I never wanted to discuss, though I understood her meaning. She looked at me after picking her sickles up. "Get your little black butt over here, and let's do it again. This time, keep that lazy left of yours higher!" She clapped the blades of her sickles twice together and stood at the ready once more.

I reluctantly walked over to my sickles and picked them up. I could tell by the way our conversation had gone, she and I would probably be at this for the rest of the day.

CHAPTER 11

Bo Daddy

Daisy was panting as she quickly made her way down a narrow game trail in the woods. She ducked and dodged the abrasive, flesh ripping branches of the huge pine trees that lined the trail. Her heart felt as if it was about to burst inside her chest. Beads of sweat poured down her forehead and cheeks; her dress soaked through with sweat, clinging to her tiny frame as if glued on. Bishop's man, musket in hand, followed closely behind, but kept his distance as to not alert her to his presence.

Daisy stopped walking and placed her back against a tall Georgia Pine to catch her breath. She remembered her sister's warning *'BE CAREFUL'* and took every precaution not to be followed. She took care to peek around the sides of the tree periodically and listen for any strange sounds. Bishop's man saw her stop and got lower, as he continued to creep towards her. Daisy noticed the crickets and critters of the woods had gone silent. She inhaled deeply through her nose and blew the breath out slowly. She looked around cautiously, then, continued up the trail.

Bishop's man continued to follow her again. He stepped over a tree that had fallen across the trail, but in his haste, inadvertently stepped onto a fallen branch causing it to snap loudly. Daisy heard the snap and began to move more rapidly through the woods. He heard Daisy's foot cadence become more rapid, and quickly pursued her. Daisy, totally out of breath, placed her hands on her knees, before looking up and seeing the smoke from Abbey Copper's chimney. Tears of fear streamed down her face mixing with sweat. She summoned the last of the strength inside her frail body and ran as fast as she could towards the smoke.

Bishop's man ran at his top speed, lumbering through the woods, clumsily swatting branches out of his way as he did. Daisy frantically ran through the woods. She ignored being hit in the face by branches, and scraped by sharp pine needles. She looked behind and saw Bishop's man gaining on her. He fell, rolled over, and jumped to his feet, in one smooth motion. He yelled to her frustrated, "When I catch you, you little bitch, I'm gonna kill you!"

Daisy continued running and crying at the same time. Just as she looked back to see where the man was, she was knocked to the ground. She hit a large muscular body of a hooded man standing in the middle of the trail. She attempted to scream, but the man quickly covered her mouth, picked her up, and ducked behind a large pine tree, all at once. Daisy struggled to break free of the man's clutches, but quickly realized he was too strong. He removed the hood from his head slowly and revealed himself to her. Much to Daisy's surprise, he was a dark, brown-skinned, strikingly handsome black man with a smooth bald head. He looked at Daisy and smiled, showing all of his perfectly white teeth, which calmed her instantly.

Bishop's man stopped and listened for Daisy's footsteps. He concentrated, listening as hard as he could, but heard only the forest birds chirping. He looked all around, but saw no sign of Daisy. Shaking his head in frustration, he pulled a small silver flask from his vest pocket, unscrewed the cap, and took a long swig. He winced from the strong whisky burning his throat as it went down, giggling afterward and talking to himself, "Shit! Bishop ain't payin me enough for all this."

He placed the cap back onto the flask and began searching for Daisy once more. He spat, then, lifted his musket into firing position down the trail. Suddenly, he thought he saw something move further up the path. He moved cautiously toward a figure. Smiling to himself, as if playing a children's game, he whispered, "I see you, you little bitch." He stalked slowly up the trail, then, suddenly burst into full sprint towards the figure. Just before reaching what he believed to be Daisy, a twig snapped under his right foot and yanked him violently off the ground.

Stunned and a bit dazed, he found himself helplessly dangling upside down. As his focus cleared, he could see his musket lying on the ground. "Shit!", he thought to himself, as he wriggled to get free. When he realized that his wriggling was in vain, he cried out, "Help me! Oh please God, help me!" He heard the sound of someone moving through the dead leaves. Frantically, he craned his head to the left and right, attempting to catch a glimpse of whoever or whatever was moving toward him.

The hooded man and Daisy calmly walked over to Bishop's man, as he dangled and bounced helplessly from the rope. He watched nervously as the hooded man and Daisy approached him. Seeing the hooded man was black, Bishop's man relaxed and cried out forcefully, "Boy, who do you belong to? Give me a hand here!" The hooded man ignored him, and picked the musket up off the ground. He began to nonchalantly inspect the weapon. Bishop's man hung there watching in disbelief. "Boy, if you don't put that musket down, there's gonna be hell to pay!"

The black man bent at the waste until he and Bishop's man were eye-to-eye. He spoke in Geechee dialect, "First all, ya seem to tink me name is boy. Let I straighten sum tings out for ya, Bukruh. Me name Bo Daddy. Now what me name, Bukruh?" Bishop's man began to tremble, as he answered nervously, "B, B, Bo Daddy."

Bo Daddy smiled widely. He stood and turned his back to Bishop's man. Daisy stood near the dangling man, scowling at him with contempt. Bo Daddy looked at her and began to interrogate the still dangling man, "Why ya be chasin' dis gal tru me woods?" Bishop's man became angry and defiant, "Nigger, if you don't cut me down from here right now, my boss is gonna tar and feather... YOUR ...NIGGER... ASS!"

Impervious to the man's threats, Bo Daddy turned calmly towards Daisy, "Wher ya be headed fer, lil one?" "I goin' yonder to Miss Abbey's house to warn Miss Nancy 'bout de white man wit his riders! Dey on her trail!", she answered innocently, then swiftly turned and started walking up the trail toward Abbey Copper's house.

Bo Daddy scratched his head quizzically as he watched Daisy walk away. He thought to himself for a moment, then yelled to Daisy, "Nancy? Do ya mean, da Black Nancy?" Daisy immediately stopped and turned back in the direction of Bo Daddy. "Yes'em, some folks call her dat, but she don't much like bein' called dat." Bo Daddy smiled again. "Me tink dat me better come wit'cha, to make sure none adese fuckers stop ya from warnin' ole Nancy. But first tings first."

Bo Daddy turned and slowly walked towards Bishop's man. He removed a shiny silver knife from the handmade leather vest that held nine others, identical to the one he just removed. Then, in one blindingly fast swipe of his right arm, he slit the man's throat. Daisy heard the hiss of air escaping his lungs through his esophagus and the gurgling of blood pooling in his throat and she almost threw up. The dying man grasped his throat desperately with both hands attempting to stop the blood gushing from his neck. He wriggled for a minute, then, his arms fell toward the ground above his head and his body went limp. Bo Daddy stood beside the man coldly, waiting for the life to leave the man's body. Calmly, he wiped the blood from his knife in the dead man's long, stringy hair. Once clean, he placed it back into the empty space on his custom leather vest. Daisy looked on in disbelief, for she had never seen a white man dispatched by a black person in her life; except of course by Black Nancy.

Bo Daddy walked toward the perplexed Daisy whistling as if he was completing some mundane task, like collecting firewood or milking a cow. She felt strange wanting to ask Bo Daddy what she wanted to, but she did anyway. "Did you have to kill him?", she asked innocently, as not to provoke him. Bo Daddy looked at her with the eyes of a seasoned killer, "No, me did not 'ave to kill em'. But me did anyway." His reply was cold. He spat on the dead man's body then took Daisy's hand, as they started up the trail together.

CHAPTER 12

Found Then Lost

Just as I suspected, momma and I practiced ALL day. At least it was over until the next time momma felt safe enough to practice. To say I was exhausted would have been a major understatement. Muscles were aching in my body I did not know I had. The smell of Miss Abbey's fried yard bird kept me motivated though, as it wafted from the kitchen window. One thing could be said about Miss Abbey that could not be said about most white women: that white woman could fry some chicken!

Miss Abbey yelled for us to wash up for dinner, and not a moment too soon. With newfound strength, I dashed to the washtub to clean off so I could eat! I was completely ready to gorge myself with all the food Miss Abbey prepared: fresh dandelion greens, hot water cornbread with honey and mouthwatering fried chicken! It had been ages since someone cooked a warm meal for us. In fact, I couldn't recall the last time since we left the Bishop plantation, we had hot vitals. But, to momma's satisfaction, I still remembered my table manners and I waited until grace was said.

"Dear Lord, we thank you for our bounty and we ask your blessings and protection on us. Amen.", Miss Abbey prayed softly.

We were eating at the table when Miss Abbey asked momma, "So where are you two headed when you leave here this time?" Momma chewed the food in her mouth thoroughly and thought to herself before answering. "I was thinking we should probably make are way up north." I was shocked, and ecstatic. So much so, I did a little dance in my chair. Momma and Miss Abbey giggled at my silliness. I could hardly contain myself. I glanced happily over at momma and gave her the biggest smile I could muster. "Really, Momma? What changed your mind?", I asked excitedly. Momma played coy. "Oh, a little birdie in the woods kinda made me see things differently."

Miss Abbey nodded her head in approval. "Well, I'll be sure and pack you some provisions for the trip." "No Abbey, you don't have to do that. You have already done so much for us. We couldn't ask for anything else", Momma said sincerely as she took Miss Abbey's hand and looked into her eyes.

Miss Abbey scoffed loudly, "That's a bunch a hoowee! What you have tried to do for your people... No, what you have done for your people is one of the bravest endeavors that I have had the privilege of witnessing." Miss Abbey stood abruptly, and walked to a small wooden dresser in the corner of her dining room. She pulled one of the top drawers out and removed a bottle of liquor from it. Turning back toward us, she proclaimed at the top her lungs,

"Hell, this calls for a celebration! Shit! Now where did I put my good goddamned sippin' glasses?"

Miss Abbey put her right hand up to her chin trying to remember where she had seen them last. After a few moments, she remembered. "Hah! I know what I did with those little fuckers!" She turned back to the dresser, bent down and pulled out another drawer. As she did, the glasses in the drawer clanked together. She raised them up one by one, into the sunlight from the window, inspecting them for cracks. Miss Abbey halted her inspection of the glasses when she saw a black man and a little black girl come out of the woods together, hand in hand. She squinted to get a better look, then turned her head slightly back to us. "We got company comin'."

Momma and I immediately jumped from our chairs and quickly made our way over to the window. Momma whispered, "Well, the little girl is a friend from the Conway place, her name is Daisy. But, I have never seen him before." I turned to miss Abbey in time to see her suspicious frown, turn into a smile. "If I'm not mistaken, that man is the infamous Bo Daddy. He's wanted by the slave owners as well; a fugitive like ya'll. He is a Geechee from around these parts. You know they say that he has no equal, when it comes to knife fightin'.

Momma and I looked at one another quizzically. "Bo Daddy?", we said in unison. Not sure why momma said it, but I thought his name sounded funny. I wanted to know what a Geechee was too. I had never heard the term used before. But it did not seem to be a very good time to ask. So I didn't.

Miss Abbey quickly made her way to the front door. She opened it and walked outside to greet Daisy and Bo Daddy. From the window, I saw Daisy and Bo Daddy wave happily to Miss Abbey. Miss Abbey waved back to them yelling,

"Hey, Mr. Bo Daddy!"

"How goes it, Miss Abbey?", he replied. Miss Abbey glanced down at a relieved Daisy.

"And who might you be, little lady?"

"I'm Daisy, Ma'am. Pleased to meet you." Daisy replied in her best English, to impress Miss Nancy. Miss Abbey smiled and said, "Daisy, that's such a pretty name." Blushing, Daisy said, "Thank you kindly, Ma'am. Miss Abbey, I need to talk to Miss Nancy 'bout... about", she correct herself, "a very important matter."

Momma, heard her name, and came out of the front door cautiously, as she always did. She scanned the woods to the left of the house, then the right. Seeing nothing, she walked to where the others were talking, but glared untrustingly at Bo Daddy. "Daisy, what in God's name are you doing here?" Daisy responded so excitedly, that she could hardly get the words out. "Miss Nancy, I came here to warn you about a white man, whose been torturin' Missy to find out where you is!" Momma's body language changed instantly as she scanned the surrounding woods once more. "White man? What white man? What does he look like?", she blurted out, all the while meticulously eyeing the woods.

"Ya see one Bukrah, ya see dem all", interrupted Bo Daddy. Momma turned her head sharply, and barked, "Mr., I don't know you, and you don't know me, and as far as I'm concerned, I can live the rest of my life with it stayin just like that. So, please, stay out of my business!" Bo Daddy stepped back and raised both his hands into the air as if surrendering. "Damn! Put ya guns away gal, me come here in peace!" Miss Abbey, attempting to cool the tension, interjected, "Come on Bo, why don't you and I go inside and have a bite to eat. Are you hungry?" He cuts his eye at the still glaring momma, "ya know, Miss Abbey, dat be da best offa me got in a long, long time." He walked over to Miss Abbey, who placed her arm around him and walked with her into the house.

Momma redirected her attention to Daisy. "Now, what did this new white man look like, child?" Daisy thought hard, "Well, he's tall and skinny... Oh! He has a nasty scar on this parta his face.", moving her finger down the right side of her face. Momma stood up straight and rigid. "That sounds like...but it couldn't be, Bishop." Daisy excitedly responded, "That's his name! Bishop! It's him and he got about ten riders with him. Before I left, I watched them torturin' Missy somethin' awful, tryin a find out where you at!"

Momma looked back at the house and said, "How did you wind up with that man in there?" Now facing Daisy, said angrily, "Did that nasty son-of-a-bitch try to touch you?" Daisy looked at momma confused, "No, Ma'am. Nothin' like that. Truth be told, if it hadn't been for Bo Daddy, I'da never made it here."

"What do you mean?", asked momma puzzled.

"Just before I got here I figured I was bein'

followed. I's sure it was one of Bishop's men. He woulda caught me if it wasn't for Bo Daddy. He caught that cracka in some kinda trap in the woods and killed him without battin' an eye."

Momma looked both surprised and impressed.

"So, Mr. Bo Daddy did all that, huh?"

"Yes, ma'am, he did", Daisy said proudly.

"So, maybe you could be a little nicer to him? For me, please, Miss Nancy?"

Momma thought to herself, and a tiny smile slowly appeared on her face. "I'll try my hardest, just for you, baby. You risked your life for me by coming here, and I will be eternally grateful." At that moment, Daisy and momma embraced as if mother and daughter. Suddenly a shot rang out from the woods-- from where I could not tell. Daisy's frail little body went limp in momma's arms. She looked into momma's eyes and with her dying breath whispered, "I love you... like you was my own momma. Don't let them catch you." Her eyes remained wide open as her arms dropped lifelessly from around momma, to her sides.

Momma stood there holding Daisy's

lifeless body in her arms. In shock, she muttered over and over to herself, "No, no, no, no!" Her face showed the anguish of a mother who had just witnessed her child's murder. She stood there motionless trying desperately to hold Daisy's head up. Tears streamed down both sides of her cheeks as she slowly lowered Daisy's body gently to the ground, as if placing a baby in a crib. Momma kissed Daisy gently on the forehead, "Thank you, sweet child."

At that moment, Bishop stepped out of the woods in front of momma with the musket he used to kill Daisy. The barrel was still smoking. He placed the butt of the musket onto his right hip and stood there smirking. "Hey Nancy! Do I have your undivided attention?"

A chill rushed down my spine as momma stood up. I could literally fill the rage building inside her. She stood stoically over Daisy's body. I could not take it anymore, I ran to the front door, and yanked it open. Yelling as loud as I could, "Momma!" She turned her head slightly without taking her eyes off Bishop and said calmly, "Ruby stay where you are, baby." I stepped back into the house as momma turned her head and attention back into the direction of Bishop. "Oh yeah! You got my attention, cracka!", Momma replied defiantly. Bishop giggled, then rebutted, "Now is that any way to talk to your master! Here is the situation; me and my boys have come a long way and at great expense, I might add, to retrieve you and your daughter. You got fifteen muskets pointed at your black ass right now. But let it not be said that I am unreasonable man. We can work this thing out!"

I strained to see how many men were actually out there while momma talked. I only saw one other man, but what I could hear scared me more than the potential for battle. Somewhere in the distance, I could here hunting dogs yelping, begging their handler to be let loose on whatever dark thing, animal or human they deemed fit. I strained my ears to distinguish how many dogs there actually were. I guessed maybe three or four. God, for once, I prayed I was exaggerating the number.

Miss Abbey watched pensively from her window for a moment, then, quickly walked over to the thickly woven round area rug on the floor in the center of the living room. With one swift yank of it, she revealed a trap door. Bo Daddy watched as Miss Abbey unveiled the trap door and smiled widely. He quickly removed the trap door and looked at me, and Miss Abbey,

"Where dis go?"

"Well, I never been down there myself... but, my Charles dug it and he said that it takes you just past the tree line into a wash about 50 yards out.", she answered without pause.

Bo Daddy jumped down into the hole, and peered down the pitch-black tunnel. Ancient cobwebs hung from the railroad tie supports of the tunnel. I summoned all of my courage. "I want to go too!" I said quickly and in my bravest voice. Bo Daddy quickly dismissed the idea. "No gal, me don't know what me walking into. So ya stay 'ere wit Miss Abbey and keep ya'self low. Okay?" I acted as if I was angry with Bo Daddy at the time, but I was actually relieved.

When I looked down into the tunnel, Bo Daddy was placing one of his knives between his teeth then disappeared into the darkness. I ran back over to the window to check on momma, who was still standing over Daisy's body, listening to the smug Bishop. "Damn! I almost forgot! I brought another one of your dear friends from your past with me!" Momma watched as a portly, old man road his horse up to where Bishop was standing. He dismounted and yelled at Bishop, "What in the hell are you doing? She's right there...kill that bitch!" The way Mr. Conway animatedly flailed his hands and arms in the direction of momma, scared me.

Bishop looked back at Conway with contempt. "You just don't get it, do you?" Conway was confused. "Get what?" Bishop walked up to Conway until they were both face to face. "This is my deal, Mr. Conway." Bishop turned back to momma who was still standing motionless in the front yard. "Now, Nancy, this is how it's gonna go. I want you to walk toward me slowly, right now."

It was as if time stood still. I swear, the wind stopped blowing and the birds stopped chirping in anticipation of something. Momma thought to herself long and hard, took a deep breath and held it. She blew the breath from her lungs slowly, then, called out to Bishop, "And if I don't?" Bishop smirked and took aim at her with his musket once more, dropping to one knee with his left eye closed and his right eye trained down the barrel. "Then I'll shoot you where you stand!", he replied.

Momma looked down at Daisy's body for a final time. Then, in seemingly one motion, she turned and started running back toward the house. Strategically, she zigzagged across the front yard. Bishop saw her and yelled for his men to fire. The woods erupted with deafening musket fire all at once. I could see the muzzle blast flames spew from their barrels, hurling deformed chunks of metal towards momma. The air quickly began to fill with white gun smoke. The smell of burnt sulfur filled the air, replacing the smell of fresh pine. Bishop himself, as well as Conway, opened fire on momma.

Miss Abbey tackled me, knocking me away from the window. We huddled together on the floor as the windows, glasses and plates randomly exploded when struck by the multiple round balls and shots. Bullets and round balls hit the side of the house, splintering the wood. Momma ran toward the window that I had been watching from. I managed to break away from

Miss Abbey in time to see momma take a bullet in the shoulder. She winced in pain, but didn't even slow down as she ran toward the house. Miss Abbey snatched me away from the window as momma, holding her shoulder, dove through the same window. Bullets shattered the glass and splintered the window casing as she landed inside the house with a thud when she hit the wooden floor. She crawled over to me and kept me safe by using her own body as a shield.

Bo Daddy quickly reached the end of the tunnel. He removed the knife from his mouth, and slowly stuck it out from the tunnel's opening until he could see the reflections of two of Bishop's men guarding their horses. The two men heard the guns being fired, and whooped and hollered. Because their backs were turned, they didn't see Bo Daddy exit the tunnel and place the knife into his pants at the small of his back. He began to nonchalantly walk toward the men as if taking an afternoon stroll in the park. Bishop's men turned and faced the direction in which Bo Daddy approached.

Once within arm's-length of the men he spoke.

"Pardon I. Could ya tell I how to get to..." and without warning, swiftly pulled the knife from his pants and sliced the throats of both men. Both of them looked at Bo Daddy in disbelief, as blood gushed from gaping wounds in their throats. He stood there watching as the men desperately grabbed for his legs with looks of disbelief on their faces. Blood trickled down the front of their shirts. Once dead, Bo Daddy confiscated their pistols, placing them into his pants. He then loosed all but four horses.

Momma, Miss Abbey and me stayed as low as we could, as Bishop and his men riddled the house with gunfire. Debris fell to the floor like snow in a winter blast. Glasses and dishes exploded and rained down on our heads. Miss Abbey's beloved picture frame, containing the only photos of her late husband and son, was knocked to the floor. She crawled on her belly frantically over to it, grabbed the frame off the floor, and held it lovingly to her heart. She closed her eyes tightly as bullets and round balls whistled overhead. I could see Miss Abbey's lips moving in silent prayer.

All of a sudden, Bishop's raspy voice

yelled for his men to stop firing. A dead silence ensued. "Hold it! Hold it! Cease fire!" he shouted to the men on both sides of him. Momma slowly raised herself off me, and sat up with her back against the wall under the window. I did the same. Bishop confidently stood out in the open, as if he had won this battle. He yelled out to momma, "Hey Nancy, you alright in there?" He removed his hat and laughed as he wiped his forehead with his left jacket sleeve. "I must say, you are goddamned impressive. Never in my life have I seen a nigger such as you. But, there is nowhere left for you to run now. So come out and save the lives of your daughter and friend!"

Mr. Conway stood next to Bishop with a sour look on his face. He turned to Bishop and spat out angrily, "I didn't come here to negotiate with that bitch!" He turned back toward a man holding four large bloodhounds. "I'll show you how to flush that bitch out. Let 'em go, Butch!" Butch began pulling the muzzles from the large hound's mouths. The dogs jumped and bayed loudly as they eagerly awaited release from their leashes. Butch pet and rubbed each dog's face vigorously, "You be good boys and get them darkies out of that house." He released all of the dogs and watched proudly as they all bolted towards the house.

"Go get 'em boys! Get some!" he yelled while clutching the leashes of his vicious dogs.

Although the deafening shooting ceased, I heard an even more horrendous sound: barking hounds! I peeked from the corner of the window. My eyes widened in fear as four huge hounds barreled towards the house, baying and lumbering across the clearing. I turned quickly to momma. "Momma, dogs!" I backed away from the window and screamed at the top of my lungs as the lead dog from the pack leaped through it, breaking through what was left of the window frame.

I felt the warm sensation of my own urine run uncontrollably down the inside of my trembling legs. Momma appeared from nowhere, and cut the dog in half with her sickle with one swing. The front half, from head to mid-section, hit me with enough force to knock me to the floor. The back half landed outside of the house onto the porch.

Miss Abbey jumped up and ran to the drawer where she kept her good sippin' glasses. She gave the side of the dresser a swift kick and a secret compartment fell open, revealing a shiny double-barreled shotgun. She quickly bent down and grabbed it.

Just as she spun around with it, two voracious hounds leaped through the same window as the leader of the pack did. Momma dove away from the window backwards as they did, sliding across the floor on her back when she hit.

Miss Abbey fired both barrels simultaneously at the invading animals, like a war veteran, determined and focused. Buckshot ripped through both of the dog's bodies while still in the air. They yelped loudly in pain as they were blown back into the front wall of the house. Their bodies hit the wood floor with a dull thud and they moved no more.

Butch, the dog handler, ran and jumped onto a fallen tree for a better vantage point to see his dogs. He was visibly shaken because he feared the worst: his dogs had been killed. He called out to the dogs, but all hope of them returning vanished, as he heard no more barking. Bishop smirked at Mr. Conway, who was tremendously frustrated and embarrassed. Bishop was much too pious to say aloud, "I told you so", yet that's just what he was thinking. In his heart, he knew he was better equipped to catch Black Nancy. Or so he thought.

All had finally grown quiet. I closed my eyes tightly, and pushed the half a dog off me onto the floor. Its warm, sticky blood covered my face, hands, and clothes. Trying to ignore the discomfort, I stood up and began blinking rapidly, trying to clear my eyes of blood. I turned to momma, raised my hands in disgust and started to sob. Momma came to my aid immediately, and used the bottom of her dress, trying to wipe the blood from my eyes. It was then, we all heard Bishop's orders as he barked them loudly to his men. "Alright boys, let's go clean em' out!"

Miss Abbey had a moment to survey her once immaculate house: it was shred to pieces. All of her knickknacks that once graced the shelves were in splintered pieces on the floor. Her dining room table, now half standing, and all the place settings were now riddled with holes. There was no longer any glass in the windows and her favorite reading lamp, next to her favorite rocking chair, now lay destroyed, next to the hearth. She pushed the sadness of the event deep down inside her and filled it with a new resolve: Abbey was finally done with this foolishness. She broke the double barrel to reload. She opened another drawer and fumbled around in it, searching for more ammunition.

Mr. Conway determined not to live with the failure of his dogs for very long, quickly made his way over to his horse and mounted him. Yanking the reins and digging his spurs deep into the flanks of the horse, he rode towards the house behind Bishop's men from a safe distance. All of Bishop's men emerged from their hiding places in trees and from behind bushes, walking into the clearing. They cautiously approached the house, each with their muskets pointed in the direction of the house.

Momma struggled to get it all, but the blood was stuck to my eyes and face like dried paint. Still blinded, I heard a thump on the floor, then a deep, menacing growl. This hound, we had not accounted for. Momma turned fearlessly to face the dog. She raised her right hand with the sickle in it towards the dog and with her left, guided me behind her, using her body to shield me. Momma said the dog trained its eyes on her, and began to slowly move towards us, while growling and baring its huge teeth.

Miss Abbey continued to fumble through the same drawer, trying to keep and eye on the dog at the same time. She finally found one shotgun shell and as quick as she could, placed it into the left barrel of the shotgun. She snapped it closed and took aim at the hound. Closing one eye, she pulled the trigger. I braced myself to hear the roar of a shotgun blast, but all I heard was a low sizzle. The shotgun shell she struggled to find was no good. Miss Abbey lowered the gun dejectedly, and watched helplessly as the vicious hound slowly stalked momma and me.

The hound bared its razor sharp canines and prepared to attack us. Momma stood at the ready in front of me motionless, studying every movement of the animal, looking for a tell of some kind on when it would attack. I took my fingernails and scraped the sticky blood from my eyes in time to see the dog leap into the air at momma. She reared back her sickle to strike, but before she had a chance to swing, a shot rang out and the hound was abruptly knocked from the air. Its lifeless carcass slid across the floor coming to a stop in front of Miss Abbey.

In shock, Momma, Miss Abbey, and I slowly turned our heads in the direction of the shot. Bo Daddy was standing in the opening of the trap door with a smoking pistol in his hand and a wide smile on his face. "Time to go, Ladies! The Bukrah dun gave Bo Daddy some horses!" I looked up at momma's face; she was frowning at Bo Daddy. Then, slowly she began to smile at him as she grabbed me under my armpits to lower me into the tunnel. It takes a lot to impress momma, but I could tell she was starting to like Bo Daddy. As she lowered me down to him in the tunnel she said gratefully, "Mr. Bo Daddy, I'm starting to like your style." Bo Daddy placed the pistol into his pants and smiled back proudly at momma. "Miss Nancy, me do have me moments. Now come." Bo Daddy reached his hand out to help momma down into the tunnel. He noticed that Miss

Abbey was not moving to the opening.

Miss Abbey walked calmly over to the tattered, brass picture frame containing the photo of her husband and son and picked it up, shaking out the broken glass. Bo Daddy became restless and called out to her, "Miss Abbey! We no time ta waste!" Miss Abbey then walked past Bo Daddy's outstretched hand. She grabbed the large bible she had been reading earlier that day, off the mantle, and sat in her now bullet riddled rocking chair. She sat there studying the photo and began to slowly rock as if it was a calm Sunday morning. Bo Daddy desperately called to her once more.

"Miss Abbey, wha'cha be doin' now?" She stopped rocking and looked over at Bo Daddy.

"Bo Daddy?"

"Yes, Ma'am", he answered respectfully.

"You be sure and get those ladies up North, you hear!"

Bo Daddy realizing that Miss Abbey would not be coming with us, answered somberly, "Yes, Ma'am, Miss Abbey. Me will." Miss Abbey proceeded to open the bible and read from it, humming her favorite spiritual. I believe it was *We're Marching to Zion.* Bo Daddy grabbed the trap door and placed it over the opening.

While Bo Daddy, Nancy and Ruby were secretly making there way through the dank tunnel, Bishop simultaneously signaled some of his men to go around to the rear of the house. One of the men peeked through a bullet whole in the front wall of the house. He saw Miss Abbey rocking calmly in her chair and reading the bible. He signaled Bishop and the others, waving his hand toward them. Bishop and the rest of his men cautiously made their way to the front of the house. He looked around to make sure his men were in position. He opened the door, which fell off its hinges. Signaling two of his men by moving his head, he told them to enter the house. Without hesitation, the two men rushed into the house with muskets aimed at Miss Abbey. One man moved to the left of the door, the other to the right. Miss Abbey, seemingly unaffected, continued to read from her bible and ignored the men pointing rifles at her. She continued humming to herself.

At this point, Mr. Conway arrived at the

front of the house. He immediately dismounted and ran into the house, brushing past Bishop's men. He looked down at Miss Abbey puzzled. Bishop entered the house and stood behind Mr. Conway. He looked around, turned to his men and said, "Search the rest of the house, and a few of you look in them woods back yonder!"

Aggressively, Mr. Conway walked up to Miss Abbey, looked down at her and scowled, "Where the hell is Black Nancy? Where is she, you nigger lovin' bitch!" Miss Abbey instantly stopped rocking. She slowly lifted her head from the bible, and stared directly at Mr. Conway as if she was trying to see into his soul. She eerily answered him with a question of her own, "Would your name be Conway?"

Mr. Conway, taken aback by her query, looked back at Bishop confused. "Yes, my name is Conway. But how would you know that?" His forehead began to crinkle as he became agitated because he realized he was answering this nigger lovin' bitch. "Listen! You better just tell us where Black Nancy has gone and you might live through this!" Miss Abbey, unimpressed, ignored him. She turned the picture frame around for Mr. Conway to see. "Mr. Conway, this was my husband Charles Copper. Does that name mean anything to you?"

At that moment, one of Bishop's men descended the stairs and shook his head at Bishop. Bishop was visibly disappointed and spat out, "Shit! She ain't here!" Suddenly another one of Bishop's men burst through the front doorway out of breath. "Mr. Bishop! I found Lewis and Todd, with their throats cut and all the horses gone!" Miss Abbey giggled to herself and began rocking her chair again. Bishop stepped outside with his man to find out what was going on.

After having pondered the name of Miss Abbey's husband, Mr. Conway turned to her and confirmed, "You know, I do seem to recall a fella by that name." Miss Abbey stopped rocking again and turned her head slowly toward Mr. Conway. With utter disgust she snapped, "You should remember, you slimy son of a bitch! It was you who strung him up, you low down piece of shit!" Without warning, Miss Abbey pulled out her husband's pepperbox pistol from her bible that was lodged between the pages and shot

Mr. Conway in the face.

Mr. Conway, with shock frozen upon his face, fell backwards to the floor with a loud thud. By all accounts, he had a perfectly circular wound between his eyes, which trickled blood down the bridge of his nose. Bishop and his men heard the gunshot and all rushed back into the house with weapons drawn. Miss Abbey instantly jumped from her rocker, stood over Mr. Conway and unloaded the remaining seven shots from her pepperbox pistol into his motionless body, with a wicked smile of satisfaction on her face.

After a few more clicks of her empty pistol, she looked up and saw Bishop and three of his men with their weapons aimed at her. Miss Abbey in her defiant way smiled widely and closed her eyes as Bishop and his men fired and cut her down. People say that all Miss Abbey ever wanted, was to avenge the death of her beloved Charles, before she left this world. And I believe she did.

CHAPTER 13

Me Billage

After escaping yet again from Bishop, Bo Daddy, Momma, and I rode our stolen horses down what used to be a red clay road. I say 'used to be' because it was overgrown with tall grass and weeds on both sides. I kept looking behind, praying not to see any sign of Bishop and his men following us. Bo Daddy led because the road was really nothing more than a path, forcing us to ride single file. I could see the thick, black puffs of smoke rising in the direction of what was once Miss Abbey's house. It saddened me deeply that she did not decide to come with us. I think I finally understand what momma meant when she would say, 'people have to follow their own destiny.'

We continued until we came to a section of road that was covered by giant, ancient oak trees. Their huge branches hung over the road, forming a living tunnel. The Spanish moss was thick and dangled so low, it brushed the tops of our heads as we road by. It was dark and humid and very difficult to see threw all the vegetation. I was tired and thirsty and terribly concerned about where we were going and if Bishop and his men were close behind.

Bo Daddy would turn to check on us periodically. He noticed momma was sweating and appeared very weak. "Ya alright, Nancy?" he asked. She managed a half-hearted smile but no more, which concerned Bo Daddy. I was too busy trying to see so I didn't notice how bad my momma really looked. Besides, Miss Abby continued to pop into my mind. I know she was ready to die, but I held out hope that she made it. She was the closest thing to a friend either me or momma ever had.

"Momma, do you think Miss Abbey made out okay?" Momma slowly turned in her saddle towards me. "I'm sure things made out the way she wanted them to-- knowing her", she said softly. I noticed how momma struggled to turn forward again in her saddle. "Momma, are you okay? You don't look so good." Momma responded weakly, "I'll be fine child." Trusting her, I continued to ramble on about Miss Abbey. "I hope Miss Abbey made it. She was a real nice lady, I mean...for a white lady." "Her being white had nothing to do with it. She was just a good person, and my only friend in this godforsaken land," Momma snapped weakly again.

Seeing Momma become agitated, I attempted to change the subject, and since I was tired of not knowing where we were going, I made up my mind to find out. I stood in the stirrups and yelled to Bo Daddy,

"Hey, Bo Daddy! Where are you taking us? We've been on this so-called road for hours!"

"Keep ya self quiet." Bo Daddy scowled, with his pointer finger to his lips. "Or do ya want da Bukruh ta eer ya?"

Annoyed, he turned forward and continued to ride. My feelings were hurt because Bo Daddy scolded me, but I understood what he meant. Still, I asked "Bukruh? Momma, what's Bukruh mean?"

"I believe it means 'white folk', in Geechee

talk" she responded.

"Oh, I remember Miss Abbey saying something about him being a Geechee. Momma, what exactly is a Geechee?" I asked again, feeling more ignorant than I ever have before. Momma, as always in her patient manner, began to answer me.

"Well, child, the Geechee's are..." Suddenly Momma's eyes rolled to the back of her skull and she began to convulse violently as she fell from her mount.

I quickly jumped down from my horse and ran over to where she lay on the ground. I cried out for Bo Daddy who was still riding up the road, unaware what was happening behind him.

"Bo Daddy! Bo Daddy! There's something wrong with momma!" I screamed to him frantically. He immediately stopped and jumped off his horse. He ran back to where Momma and I were, and placed his hand onto Momma's forehead.

"My God, she be burnin' up", he said. He noticed a bloodstain on momma's left shoulder so he rolled her body onto its right side. That's when we saw it-- a minie ball hole in the shoulder of her dress. He reached into the circular hole with two of his fingers and ripped it open revealing a festering wound in her shoulder. Bo Daddy looked at me grimly.

"Tis no good, Lil One. She need elp."

"You gotta help her, Bo Daddy! You gotta help my momma! Bo Daddy, please!" I pleaded with him.

I started crying uncontrollably, as I lifted momma's head from the ground and placed it onto my lap. I began to brush her face with my hand trying to console her, and trying to conceal my own fear. "Don't worry, Momma, I'm gonna take care of you."

Bo Daddy hurried over to his horse and grabbed a canteen from the saddlebag. He turned and scanned the surrounding trees, as if searching for something. He ran over to a low hanging branch with a large amount of Spanish moss hanging from it, and grabbed a handful. He turned back quickly towards us kneeling down next to momma. I watched him, unsure of what he intended to do. He reached under momma's dress and ripped some material from beneath it.

He then took the moss he gathered and placed it into the material he had ripped from her dress. Removing the top from the canteen, he wet the Spanish moss inside of the dress material and looked up at me. "Lift ha careful."

I braced my hands against momma's back and pushed her into a seated position. Bo Daddy placed the material with the moss onto the wound in momma's shoulder and tied it into place with straps of leather from the saddlebags. Momma regained semi-consciousness for a moment and began to moan a bit. I noticed a trickle of blood down her forehead from where she hit her head in the fall from her horse. She looked up at me, and smiled before loosing consciousness again. "You are gonna be alright, momma," I said comfortingly to her.

Bo Daddy lifted momma gently off the ground and laid her across the saddle on her horse. He turned to me, with determination in his eyes, and said, "We ave to move fast, or da Black Nancy no make et." With the fear of loosing the only person in this entire world that gave a damn about me, I impatiently responded, "Let's go to wherever we need to. Fast!" I ran over to my horse and jumped onto its back in one motion ready to ride. "Let's go, Bo Daddy. Where can we go?" Bo Daddy grabbed the reins of the horse that momma was on and remounted his own. "We go to da only place I know dey can elp er. We go to me billage." Bo Daddy and I kicked the flanks of our mounts and headed toward wherever this village was.

CHAPTER 14

Smelliest Man On Earth

Bishop and his men rode in a single file line, down the same skinny road we had been traveling not more than a few hours earlier. At the head of the column rode a tracker of some renown in Georgia, named Daniels. He was believed to have Indian blood in him. All I knew of him was his reputation for being maybe the smelliest man on God's green earth. Bishop rode closely behind him holding a scarf up to his face, in an attempt to combat the stench of Daniels.

Bishop, dressed in his signature black duster, waited with bated breath for Daniels to find some trace of where, and in what direction we had escaped. Daniels rode slouched forward, with his eyes locked on the trail, like the many hounds that have tracked my people. He periodically switched from staring at the left side of the road to the right. It was after one of his periodic switches he noticed an indentation in the ground. He stopped and quickly dismounted.

Walking slowly over to the spot where momma had fallen from her horse to the ground, he turned back. "Mr. Bishop, they definitely come this way. They stopped here, then changed direction and went off to the east toward the coast. Oh, and one more thang, one of em' is bleedin' real bad," he spoke softly, with a deep southern drawl but with great confidence. Then, he spat a disgusting, gooey wad of chewing tobacco from his mouth. Remnants of tobacco and spit oozed down the front of his chin.

Bishop thought to himself, as he looked off into the direction of the coast, then asked, "How far ahead would you say they are, Daniels?" Daniels bent down and grabbed some dirt from inside a footprint on the road. He threw some of it into his mouth and swirled it around, then spat it back out onto the ground. He turned back to Bishop and answers confidently. "I'd say about a day, Mr. Bishop." "Are you sure?" Bishop asked seriously, with a bit of uncertainty in his voice. He stared at Daniels as if his life depended on his next statement. Daniels walked over to Bishop and looked up at him; offended that Bishop would even question his findings. "As sure as can be, Mr. Bishop." Bishop broke out into a smile and turned to the rest of his men. "Alright boys! We'll camp here tonight and catch the magnificent Black Nancy tomorrow." He turned back to Daniels, reached into his vest pocket and flicked him a gold piece for his work.

CHAPTER 15

A Place Without Whips And Chains

Bo Daddy, Momma and I, road out of what seemed to be an endless entanglement of woods and weeds. We exited the thicket onto what I can only describe as the most beautiful piece of land I have ever laid eyes on. Mounds of white, powdery sand dunes dotted the coastline. Giant rolls of buttermilk colored waves crashed against the beach, one after the other, like a rhythmic dance being displayed for all to enjoy. The sound of its dance rivaled the loudest thunderclaps I had ever heard. The smell of fresh salty air filled my nose and the wind blew my hair strait back as if I was still riding my horse or running as fast as I could. It was wondrous. Although, I knew Bishop and his men were hot on our heels, I felt a strange sense of calm for some reason.

Momma groaned, which brought me back from my daydreaming. I rubbed her back from atop of my horse. Bo Daddy pulled the reins of the horse Momma was riding and we continued down the beach. A few miles further up the beach, I saw another sight I had never seen: Three Geechee Fishermen out in the ocean, I think, in traditional handmade boats. One of them cast a net into the ocean. I also saw a different boat with only one Geechee man in it. He was hauling in a sizable catch from the ocean.

We trotted our horses a little farther up the beach, that's when I saw it: The Geechee Enclave. We approached the enclave slowly. There were many black men and women wearing garments that I had never seen before. I wasn't sure, but their clothing reminded me of some of the stories Momma had told me about, much like what she wore in her homeland.

As we road in, the people from the enclave turned and watched us. There was so much to take in. Hundreds of questions flooded my mind all at once: Where was their master? Where are the cotton fields? Where is the big house? Where was their overseer? Where were their slave quarters? All I saw were huts made from mud and the seashells I saw strewn everywhere on the beach. I also saw an elderly man smoking from a handmade pipe as he hand-mended one of his fishing nets, as if he had not a care in the world. A few steps away from the old man I saw two girls, about my age, husking rice by simultaneously thrusting two large poles into a wooden container filled with wild rice. The both of them stopped working abruptly to watch us ride pass. My head was about to burst from it all. I felt like I was in a dream.

It was dusk and the light was beginning to fade, but the enclave was well lit by many torches hanging on each individual hut, with a huge communal fire pit at its center. I could here the sound of someone hard at work banging away on some metal object of some kind. Must have been the village blacksmith.

Bo Daddy halted his horse in front of the hut where the blacksmith was working. He was a huge, very dark-skinned man, built like no black man I had ever seen before. His body and face were covered in thick dripping sweat. Every muscle and tendon in his arms became visible as he struck the metal. His chest was as wide as a water barrel. Sparks flew into the air with every strike of his hammer upon the metal.

Bo Daddy dismounted and walked into the blacksmith's hut. The blacksmith struck the metal once more, looked up and saw Bo Daddy walking into his hut. He scowled angrily at him, paused his hammer, then looked back down at the metal and continued to work, ignoring him.

I was distracted by several of the enclave's children who walked over to my horse to study us curiously. I smiled at them, and they all waved to me shyly. I waved back to them, wondering what they thought. Many of the adult enclave members began to gather around Momma and I, as curious as the children. They shuffled amongst themselves, pointing and whispering words I couldn't understand.

Meanwhile, Bo Daddy stood in the blacksmith's hut with his arms extended toward the blacksmith, as if waiting for an embrace. But the blacksmith continued to act as if Bo Daddy wasn't there. He just pounded away at the metal a few more times then suddenly stopped. He placed his hammer onto the table directly behind him, and grabbed a large pair of clamps.

Using the clamps to grab the glowing red-hot piece of metal, he dunked it into a large barrel filled with water. It sizzled loudly as it was cooled by the water, and bellowed a thick white plume of steam into the air. He once again looked up at Bo Daddy with the utmost contempt. Bo Daddy realized he was not welcome and turned slowly and walked out of the hut.

I dismounted and walked over to check on momma. I stood next to her and her horse as more and more people from the enclave gathered around us. I was becoming a bit nervous, but felt relieved when I saw Bo Daddy. His head hung as he walked dejectedly out of the blacksmith's hut. Once he looked up, he saw all of the people gathered around us. When the Geechees saw Bo Daddy, they began to whisper his name.

He walked to where I was standing with the reins of momma's horse in my hands and carefully pulled momma down from the horse. He held her limp body in his arms as if she were his bride and turned to the people:

"Dis women needs elp! She need a Grannie, or she don't make it! She been shot by da Bukruh! Ya muss elp ha!" He implored. By this time, many more people had gathered around us. They had begun to whisper even more.

The blacksmith came out of his hut, still with a bitter scowl on his face. He walked toward Bo Daddy. "You are da same troublemaka dat ya always been! What for ya bring these Comeyahs to da billage for? If dis woman been shot by da Bukruh, she bring nuttin' but trouble to da people! Go from ere!" The blacksmith said boisterously, as he pointed aggressively in the direction he wanted us to leave.

Bo Daddy stood there listening to the blacksmith's rant, biting his lip. He had had enough. He turned to the people. "If we Geechee don't elp er, den I shamed to call me self one." At that moment, a boy my age left the group and ran towards the largest structure in the entire enclave. The blacksmith walked in front of Bo Daddy while he was still holding momma in his arms. "I don't care who dis woman be. I tell ya all, she ain't nuttin' but trouble for da resta us!"

He once again pointed in the direction we had come from, "Now go!"

I began to cry uncontrollably because I knew without help from a doc for Momma, she was without a doubt going to die. Overcome with emotion, I suddenly felt a rush of anger, the likes of which I had never experienced. With everything in my being I exploded. "After what my momma has done for the likes of you! You're going to send her out in the woods to die, like some... like some, animal!? Well, I say, to hell with all of you!"

Bo Daddy started to put momma back onto the horse as I glared furiously at everyone who had gathered. At that moment, I saw the same boy from earlier forcing his way back through the crowd assisting a beautiful elderly Geechee woman, with long grey locks as long as her body, and a Gris-gris bag around her neck. The boy led her to Bo Daddy as he held momma. She reached out and felt momma's forehead. "Dis woman eer is special. She risk er life ever' day for we. So, I say it for we to elp er. Take er to da Kunda now, before it be too late!"

Four of the largest male Geechee

villagers stepped out from the crowd and took momma's limp, unconscious body from Bo Daddy. Quickly, they made their way to the large structure, what the elderly woman called the Kunda. Elated Momma was going to get the help she needed, I turned to Bo Daddy for a reassuring look, but all I saw was he and the blacksmith exchanging evil looks. The blacksmith, frustrated, sighed and returned to his hut. Bo Daddy turned to me slowly and shot that reassuring look I was searching for, relieved that momma was going to get her wound tended. I think Bo Daddy was almost as worried as I was. He surprised me with a tight hug and a comforting smile. He placed his arm around my shoulders as we walked toward the Kunda.

Every member of the enclave, with the exception of the blacksmith, followed us. Spontaneously, they began to sing in a way I had never heard before. It seemed to be in a different language. They began to clap their hands and stomp their feet in unison. I turned to Bo Daddy quizzically. "Bo Daddy, what are they doing?" Bo Daddy looked down at me. "It be Geechee Shout singing. It be like ya spirituals, 'cept wit ancestral speak; wit some Geechee flare. It be how we Geechees pray, an a'time talk to each uder from afar off. Da billage pray for da Black Nancy to live."

I smiled up at him and watched the people praying in their own fashion for Momma. I remember thinking to myself, 'What a wonderful place this is. A place without whips and chains; more importantly, blacks with their own way of life and customs still here in America.' I must admit, if I was dreaming, I didn't want to ever wake from it.

CHAPTER 16

June 29, 1724

Momma lay helplessly on her back, naked from the waist up. Her body and face were covered in sweat, while she shivered with fever. She awoke briefly to the strong, mature face of Queen Molley, the one that seemed to command the most respect from all the Geechees. Momma was startled to be surrounded by strangers and attempted to sit up, but was quickly grabbed by two Geechee women who were assisting Queen Molley in removing the minie ball from her shoulder. She looked around the room deliriously. The two assistants laid momma back down onto the table very gently. Queen Molley dipped a rag into a small, wooden basin of water and wiped the sweat from momma's face. "Ya burn up, gal. Tis a good ting ya come to we when ya did." She said in a soothing voice. She inspected the wound further. Queen Molley then turned to the operating tools which she had sitting on a small table beside her. The tools consisted of a small ceremonial knife and a small metal spoon. She picked up the knife and began to cut my momma's flesh. Momma quivered in pain and passed out again. Both of Queen Molley's assistance began to chant.

Bo Daddy and I heard the women chanting. I was so confused. I didn't know what to think. It was obvious from the look on his face that Bo Daddy was just as scared as me. Besides, there was nothing else we could do. So we paced back and forth outside of the Kunda, anxiously awaiting for some word on Momma's condition. "Bo Daddy, do you think that lady knows what she's doing?" He shot me his best reassuring smile and asked, "Ya tink I bring ya all dis way if she don't? Don't ya fret yaself gal, ya mudda in da best ands she can be, belie dat." I only felt a little better. "How did you know about this place? And why does that blacksmith hate you so much?" He looked up into the night sky, which was full of bright stars, and reminisced for a moment. He sighed, then, gave me his answer.

"Dis billage... I knew of dis billage cause, Bo Daddy be from dis billage. Bo Daddy leave dis place long ago. I be da same age as you. The Bukruh come and take what dey want from we, and we had to let dem."

With a sorrowful expression on his face, Bo Daddy slowly walked over and sat on the steps of the Kunda. I walked over and sat beside him as he continued. "Dey would take da young ones--da gals-- into da woods and have dey way wit dem. One night, dey come for me little sista. Dey take er to da woods, but Bo Daddy not let that appen to him kin." Suddenly, he choked up and his eyes swelled with tears. "So what did you do?" I asked, as I hung on every word of his story.

"Bo Daddy done what him tink was right. Me grabbed me knife and went to da woods to find him little sista. I find her and all da Bukruh were still putting dem filthy ands upon her. Bo Daddy cut all dey eathen throats and cut dem manhood from dem bodies. Bo Daddy tink he save him sista, but da next day, the Bukruh come back looking for we, but, Bo Daddy long gone." I let out a big sigh of relief. "Whew. Well, at least you got away." With tears rolling down his cheeks, he finished his tale.

"Yes, Bo Daddy get away, but the Bukruh take him little sista in him place. Dey beat her wit ax handles, in da center of da billage, for all to see what appen when you stand up ta dem. The Bukruh break every tiny bone in her little body, den, hung her from dat tree." He pointed to a large tree with many hanging branches.

"Me brudda never forgive Bo Daddy for dis. Ever!"

"Your brother?" I asked, feeling a little uncomfortable, seeing his pain. Bo Daddy stood and began to walk away from me.

"Yes, me brudda. Da blacksmith-- he be me brudda," he answered dejectedly as he disappeared into the darkness of the woods. Finally, I was able to decipher his words and felt all the worse for it.

As I watched Bo Daddy disappear into the woods, I was startled by Momma's agonizing screams. The sound pierced the serenity of the night, like a needle in my eyes. I jumped and ran as fast as I could, right up to the front door of the

Kunda. With my right hand preparing to yank the door open, an unfamiliar voice called out to me in Geechee, "Hey der, gal, where ya tink ya be goin now?"

I turned to see who dared try and stop me from going to check on my mother, after all, these people were strangers to us. I swung myself quickly into the direction the voice had come from, and much to my surprise, it turned out to be the young boy from earlier, who was kind enough to get the head woman for us to look at momma's injury.

He trotted towards me smiling, with two wooden plates of food in his hands. I walked toward him, "I can't take this waiting. I really don't know what I'd do if I lost my momma." I tried to hold it in, but I couldn't and I just broke down right there.

"Ya can't be talking like dat gal. Ya momma da toughest, fiercest lady I eva 'earda. Da Queen know what she do, and da rest... Well, dat be up to da ancestors. Whetha or not dey be wantin' her to come ome. None a dat matta. It be outta ya hands now. I bring ya some food, while ya wait. Eat dis, it a make ya feel betta." He handed me the plate. I wiped my eyes and took the plate from his hand. He was right about one thing, I was starving!

I sat down right there on the steps and began to dig into the food on the plate with my fingers. The boy watched me tearing into that plate of food with a smirk on his face. He slowly took a seat next to me and started to eat as well.

"Thank you for the food. I didn't realize how hungry I was," I blurted out while still chewing.

"No problem, gal" He responded while also chewing his food. I stopped eating for a moment.

"First thing you need to know is that my name is not 'gal'. It's Ruby!" I snapped at him. He smiled uncaringly and retorted, "Ahhh, Ruby, da name. It suit cha."

Offended, I snapped at him once more. "What do you mean, the name suits me?" He placed his plate by his foot and giggled at me. "Relax ya'self ga...I mean Miss Ruby. I jus mean dat it's da name of a precious jewel."

Feeling absolutely embarrassed, I blushed and smiled uncontrollably. "Oh, in that case, thank you. What's your name?" He stood up and wiped his hands on his pants to clean them. "Me name be Timothy, and I be at ya and ya mudda's service." His manners rather shocked me and I giggled into my hand. Regaining my composure, so I wouldn't embarrass him, I teased, "You didn't have to do all of that...Timothy, but it's good to meet you." I said with a wide smile and my hand extended. He took my hand and pointed to my smile. "Oh, ya see, ya got a beautiful smile. Ya shud smile at I more of'fen."

We picked our plates up again and began to eat. This time he and I would catch ourselves sneaking looks at the other. I had the strangest feeling in my stomach; it felt like butterflies fluttering around my insides. It was weird-- but good at the same time. We were enjoying each other's company, when the voice of a Geechee woman on the other side of the enclave pierced the night. It was the voice of Timothy's mother. "Tiiii-moooo-thhhhy! Tiiiime tooo cooomme iiiinnnnnnn!" The voice said with authority.

Instantly, Timothy became nervous and dropped his plate. He picked it up and began to move towards his mother's voice. I laughed at how awkward he was moving. Thinking back on it, I found it very cute. "Well, we see ya tommora, Miss Ruby!" Timothy said as he turned and began sprinting home. I looked down and saw he had left his plate in his haste. "Hey! You forgot your plate!" He stopped abruptly and ran back to get the plate. I giggled at him again, then looked into his big beautiful brown eyes and lost myself in them. He looked into mine as well. For that fleeting moment, nothing else around us mattered. I smiled and so did he. Then he turned and sprinted away toward his hut again.

I watched him run all the way to his hut. Timothy's mother was an overweight, dark-skinned woman with long hair, wearing a really colorful apron. She waited for him just outside the front of their hut, slapping him in the back of the head as he passed her to go in. I thought it was the cutest thing I had ever witnessed.

CHAPTER 17

Whistling Dixie

After scarfing down the rest of the food Timothy brought me, I stood to stretch, enjoying the fullness in my belly. Standing outside of the Kunda alone, suddenly I had the strangest feeling-- I was being watched. An eerie chill ran down my spine and goose bumps appeared on my arms. One of the women assisting Queen Molley came out to tell me about momma's condition. I attempted to listen, but I could feel someone's eyes on me. I scanned the woods over her right shoulder, pretending to listen intently. I peered as hard as I could through the darkness, in the direction Bo Daddy only moments ago had disappeared into. I whispered a silent prayer that he was okay.

Bishop's tracker, Daniels, was in fact watching from the woods. He slowly backed away from the tree where he had been hiding. As he turned slowly, feeling pleased with his tracking abilities, he found Bo Daddy staring at him in silence. Calmly he addressed Daniels.

"It be a fine night for a stroll, Sir... don't ya tink?"

Daniels slowly pulled his knife from its sheath on his right hip. "Boy, I'm gonna cut you too short to shit, if you don't move outta my goddamn way!" Bo Daddy lowered his head and laughed sinisterly. Slowly, he raised it again, as his smile became a scowl. Bo Daddy slowly opened his jacket to reveal the custom leather harness with his eight glimmering silver knives. Each knife had its own individual pocket, four on both sides. He looked at Daniels confidently, and calmly said, "Me got eight ways for ya ta die, Bukruh. Choose one."

Daniels spat on the ground in front of Bo Daddy. Unimpressed, he started toward Bo Daddy's left side. Bo Daddy held his jacket open with both hands behind his back, like a matador, as he moved smoothly to Daniels' left. The two of them moved in a circle, stalking one another like big cats ready to pounce. Without warning, Daniels barreled forward, swinging his knife at

Bo Daddy wildly. Bo Daddy skillfully blocked Daniels' knife, by pulling one of his knives invisibly fast from the left side of his harness. Daniels was amazed at the speed and ease Bo Daddy blocked his attack.

Afraid, he backed away from Bo Daddy, not as confident as before. Bo Daddy sensing Daniels fear simply smiled at him. "Ya be scared now, huh Bukruh?" He said slyly.

Daniels summoned the rest of his courage and attacked Bo Daddy once more, swinging wildly, and screaming like a madman. Bo Daddy pulled another knife from the right side of his harness. With a knife in each hand, he blocked each wild swing of Daniels, while slowly backing away. Sparks flew each time he blocked a strike of Daniels' knife. Finally, Bo Daddy stopped Daniels' attack cold. He looked deeply and determined into Daniels' eyes and said resolutely, "It be me turn now, Bukruh."

Bo Daddy attacked Daniels with a barrage of knife strikes. The fighting triggered something in him and his mind conjured up images of his sister dangling from the tree in the village; the noose around her tiny neck; her tiny bludgeoned body. His eyes narrowed. His breathing slowed. He had the look of a determined killer.

Daniels, overwhelmed by the velocity of Bo Daddy's attack, began to back away rapidly, barely able to defend himself against the onslaught. Bo Daddy swung the knife in his left hand and successfully sliced Daniels across his chest, leaving a deep bloody gash. He envisioned the white men beating his little sister with ax handles, and the awful sound the wood made each time it hit her body, breaking her tiny bones. The images of this enraged him further. He yelled in fury and attacked Daniels even harder. Daniels backed away from Bo Daddy until he was stopped abruptly by an oak tree at his back. Sensing the inevitability of his defeat, he threw his knife to the ground and raised his hands slowly in surrender, giving Bo Daddy a sheepish look.

Bo Daddy stopped attacking and glanced down at Daniels' knife. His eyes full of rage and his heart beat so hard he could hear its beat in his head. Lathered in sweat and still breathing heavily, Bo Daddy turned his back to Daniels.

He closed his eyes and saw images of his sister and many of the young girls from the village being violated that day. He was so lost in his own thoughts that it appeared that he had forgotten all about Daniels.

Daniels, seeing an opportunity, bent down slowly and picked his knife up from the ground. He stood upright and, as quietly as he could, attempted to creep up on Bo Daddy from behind.

Bo Daddy smirked, suddenly turned and threw both of his knives in one motion. He turned around just in time to see Daniels standing in shock, mouth wide open, with one knife stuck in his throat, and the other, lodged deep into his genitals. Daniels attempted to speak. He strained to form words, but with his vocal cords severed, was unable to utter a sound. Finally, Daniels fell face first into the dirt.

Bo Daddy calmly walked to where Daniels had fallen in time to here the last of Daniels' breath leave his body. After that, he calmly turned the body over to collect his knives, grabbed Daniels by his feet, and dragged his body deep into the woods, whistling Dixie.

CHAPTER 18

Just Hold Me

The next morning, I was awakened by Geechee Fishermen chanting in unison on their way to their fishing grounds. I had fallen asleep on the top step of the Kunda. I sat up and stretched my arms above my head. As I turned my neck to stretch, I saw Bo Daddy sound asleep on the bottom step of the Kunda.

His mouth was wide open as he snored loudly. I felt relieved to see him safe. Rubbing my eyes, I shook Bo Daddy awake. He stood and began to adjust his clothing, still a little disoriented. He immediately noticed three young Geechee girls walking past the Kunda staring at him. He smiled widely at them flirtatiously. The girls turned to one another and giggled. Bo Daddy turned to me still wearing his wide smile. "Ya know, it be a whole lot more of dem women folk eer dan me remember," he said, rubbing the top of his head in a circular motion.

Queen Molley walked out of the Kunda wiping the blood off her hands with a colorful rag. Her eyes where the color of persimmons and she was moving at a turtle's pace. I knew she must have been exhausted. Bo Daddy and I rushed over to her.

"How is she? Is she gonna live? Please tell me that she's gonna be fine. Please!" I sobbed as I turned and hugged Bo Daddy. Queen Molley answered in dog-tired, monotone voice. "We got da metal out her shoulda but, da wound be infected. Me try everyting me know. Da rest be up to da ancestors." She rubbed my back like a mother comforting her child. "Ya mudda is very strong. If anyone be able ta survive dis, it be her. Ya go and see her."

I wiped my eyes and looked up at Bo Daddy. He looked down at me and gave me one of those "everything's-gonna-be-alright" looks. I took a deep breathe, dusted my clothes off and walked slowly toward the entrance of the Kunda. I wanted to rush in and hug momma, but I was so afraid of what I might see..., then I saw

Momma lying unconscious, face down on a table. My feet felt like they was stuck in mud. The air seemed thick and stale. It smelled of dried blood, sweat, and smoke; absolutely suffocating.

The two women who assisted Queen Molley busied themselves with the cleaning of the Kunda, removing the bloody rags and blood filled water basins. They both stopped when they realized I was there. They gathered their things and walked towards me. Each one gently touched my shoulder, consolingly, as she left.

My eyes filled with tears as I walked over to Momma. I took her hand and rubbed it against my cheek. I saw the bullet wound in her shoulder. It had been cleaned and stitched excellently with black thread. I bent down close to her ear and whispered "Momma, I know you can hear me. You have to come back for me, like you always do. I need you here with me. The Lord can't take you away, after everything we've been through together. It can't end like this. Me and you are going up north..." I forced a giggle. "Huh, wait till them crackas see the two of us walking down the middle of them big ole paved streets you told me about. Remember? God All Mighty, is that gonna be a sight."

I kissed Momma's hand as if it was the last time I would have a chance to do so, and gently placed it back onto the table. Not knowing what else to say or do, I just hung my head, and walked dejectedly out of the Kunda. When I stepped outside, I found Bo Daddy and Timothy waiting.

"How is ya mudda, Darlin?" Bo Daddy quickly quipped. I took a deep breath and answered him as honestly as I could. "She looks bad, Bo Daddy. Real bad!" I broke completely down and fell to my knees, bursting into tears. Bo Daddy rushed over to me and lifted me back onto my feet. "Come on now, gal, you got to be stronga dan dat, for ya mudda. Tears won't be elpin ha now."

Timothy stood behind me, awkwardly waiting for his turn to talk. Bo Daddy kissed me on top of my head, looked into my face and smiled. "Dere is someone who really wishes to ave a word wit cha. Me be back. Me gonna scare us up some breakfast." He turned and walked down the steps.

Still feeling the need for consoling, I turned my attention to Timothy. I walked over and hugged him tightly. I felt his body tense up immediately. He slowly relaxed and placed his strong arms nervously around me. "Wa wa, why are ya oldin me like dis". He stuttered.

I reared my head back to look into his face angrily. "Why? You don't like me holding you?" He stumbled over his words. "Me don't say dat. Me like holdin ya a lot, so..." I quickly interrupted. "Boy, just hold me. You ain't gotta say nothing. I just want to be held. Is that alright with you?" He buried his head into my shoulder and closed his eyes. "Yeah, Ma'am, it be fine wit me."

Suddenly, we heard the all-powerful voice of Timothy's mother. "Tiiii-moooo-thhhhy!" His eyes opened quickly as he released me and jumped off the steps of the Kunda in the direction of his hut. He looked back at me as he ran and tripped over a section of log on the ground next to the large fire pit. With nothing injured but his pride, he jumped back up and brushed the sand from his arms and legs. He smiled widely at me and yelled, "Me see ya later!" He turned once more and ran to his hut where his mother was waiting for him outside. Once again, she slapped him in the back of the head as he passed her to go into the hut. It was nice to have a diversion.

I decided to stretch my legs a little, instead of moping in front of the Kunda. I started walking through the center of the village, where I saw the blacksmith stop in front of his work hut. He lifted a large, swinging, burlap flap up and placed a thick wooden support under it. I started to wish him a 'Good morning', until he glared and scowled at me, freezing the words in my throat. I felt uncomfortable and lowered my head, turned and walked back toward the Kunda.

Bo Daddy was talking to a Geechee woman holding a sweetgrass basket full of fresh fish. When he saw me with my head hung low, he excused himself and ran up behind me and shouted excitedly, "Me just talk dat woman into makin I and ya some fish!" I didn't raise my head or respond in any way. "What's wrong wit cha, baby gal?" I snapped my head up to him aggravated. "It's that brother of yours! He is always staring at me... like... like he wants to kill me or something. Bo Daddy's demeanor changed instantly. "Is dat so? Me'll be right back." He abruptly turned and made a beeline for the blacksmith's hut.

Bo Daddy entered the hut, kicking the support out from under the front flap. It came down with a loud thud. The blacksmith spun around and faced Bo Daddy swiftly. "I tought I tole ya, you and ya two problems ain't welcome ere! You're nuttin but trouble! Ya'll bring nuttin but pain and suffrin to all who know ya!"

Bo Daddy glared back at the blacksmith, and retorted, "Me can do nuttin to bring back our baby sista! I wish I could and I wish we could be bruddas again, but ya never will forgive I for doing what me tink was da right ting-- protect me own blood! Me can't shuffle and bow to da Bukruh. Me die before me do dat again!"

The blacksmith smirked arrogantly and rebutted, "Well death is exactly what ya headed for! Ya always were wild and head strong, and now ya be travelin around wit da likes of da Black Nancy? It be only a matta of time before the Bukrah track her down. If you don't get dose women outta here by tomorrow morn, I'll trow dem out of dis billage meself!"

Bo Daddy scowled as he slowly walked toward the blacksmith, until they were practically nose to nose. Speaking intensely, he said, "Me don't care what ya do ta I... but, if ya make baby gal more scared dan she already be..."

Right then, the blacksmith cut his eyes to the right, looking at a large, black, iron hammer hanging on the wall with his other tools. Bo Daddy noticed it. "Ya gonna need dat fuckin ammer, me brudda! Me promise ya!" Bo Daddy backed away slowly, while never loosing eye contact with the blacksmith. Once at the front flap, he turned, lifted it, and left the hut.

CHAPTER 19

The Conjurer

The next morning Bishop and his men prepared to leave their campsite. His men busied themselves striking tents and rolling their bedrolls up. Bishop stood by the campfire drinking coffee from a tin cup. Steam rose from inside the cup, into the cool morning air. A few more of his men were saddling their horses. Bishop took a final sip from his cup, as he thought to himself silently. He threw the remaining coffee into the campfire, which sizzled and caused thick white smoke to plume from it.

"Ole Daniels should've been back by now. We'll just have to assume that he caught up with ole Nancy, huh."

He walked over to his horse and mounted it. Looking down, he noticed that one of his men was still asleep comfortably under the warmth of his bedroll. Bishop threw his cup at the sleeping man as hard as he could and struck the sleeping man in the forehead making a dull clunking sound. The man instantly awoke from his slumber and rubbed his head vigorously where the cup had hit him. He looked around the camp at the other men angrily. "Who the fuck hit me in the goddamned head?" The man said furiously.

Bishop spat on the ground and scowled at the man. "You get your peckawood ass up! We're goin to the coast!" The man instantly sprang to his feet, tripping over himself as he hurried to pick his things up in preparation to go.

Meanwhile, at the enclave, I watched from an open window at the rear of the Kunda, careful not to make any noise. I know I should not have, but I had to know what they were doing to help my mother. What I saw, to this day baffles me to no end:

Queen Molley and eight other Geechee women held hands as they encircled the table on which momma lay unconscious on her back. The women were all in a trance-like state. They chanted in a strange African Dialect. A small, frail dark-skinned woman entered the Kunda. She looked ancient; her skin was extra wrinkled and her body, very thin. She was known to the Geechees only as the Conjurer. No one knew where she had come from. Geechee legend had it that she had been around their enclave since its inception. She had been, since the time, before time, before time.

The Conjurer began to whisper a chant that was different from the others. She raised both her hands to the sky as she shuffled her way toward Momma. The Conjurer made her way to where Queen Molley was chanting with the other women. As if she could feel the Conjurer's presence, Queen Molley released the woman's hand on her right to allow the Conjurer to enter the circle. Once inside the Conjurer stopped and looked down at Momma's motionless body. The women suddenly stopped chanting in unison.

The Conjurer held her arms over top of Momma and shook them violently as she chanted with her eyes closed tightly. It was then two more women entered the Kunda, one carrying a live chicken, and the other a bottle of liquor of some kind. They were both dressed in all black and wore veils of the same color over their faces. They walked slowly toward the table, one directly behind the other. When they reached the other women, they were both allowed to enter the circle as well. The woman holding the chicken passed it to the Conjurer over momma's body. The chicken flapped its wings violently and crowed loudly as the Conjurer grabbed it, loosing a few of its feathers. She began to move the chicken over momma's body. First her head, then her torso, and finally over her legs.

The second woman then passed the bottle of liquor across Momma's body to the Conjurer, who took it as she held the chicken under her right armpit. The Conjurer took a long swig of the liquor, smashed the bottle on the floor, and held the chicken over Momma's body by the neck.

She spat the contents in her mouth onto the chicken. After that, she produced a knife-- I still do not know from where--it seemed from midair. The blade had all sorts of ritualistic carvings on it. Then, with one swift motion, she cut the neck of the chicken while chanting. Its blood sprayed onto momma's body. The women in the circle began to chant even louder then before. That is when I saw it, had I not seen it with my own two eyes, I would have never believed it.

Momma's once motionless body began to convulse wildly. The Conjurer raised her head and arms to the sky and chanted loudly. All of the women in there began to chant feverishly, then suddenly, they fell to dead silence and Momma's body stopped convulsing as quickly as it had started. The Conjurer shrieked and fell onto momma's body. Her two assistants calmly picked her up and carried her out over their heads silently.

Queen Molley and the other women walked around Momma. One by one, they touched her wound as they passed. Bo Daddy walked into the Kunda as Queen Molley and the other women quietly left. He approached Momma slowly. As he looked down at her he saw a small basin of water sitting on the floor. He removed the rag from it and began to gently wipe away the blood from Momma's body.

"It be time for ya to be gettin up now. Ya baby gal needs da love of her mudda, and I tired of her lookin at me, like me be da almighty imself," he said softly then laughed at himself. "Da trute be, dat me... dat me, tink ya be very special. Me neva meet anyone like ya, ever and ya know, me tink me never will. So if ya can eer me, way out dere in da darkness, me will be eer waitin for ya, till ya get back."

He dropped the rag back into the basin, backed away from momma, and knelt beside her on the floor. He looked into the sky and made something resembling the sign of the cross with his hand, then stood, turned toward the door and saw me standing in the doorway.

My eyes were full of tears watching him. I ran over and embraced him tightly. We stood there and held one another until... "You both need to quit all that goddamned cryin! Them crackas can't take me out that easy!" Momma sat up, facing Bo Daddy and I. It was a miracle. In utter shock, I ran over to momma and we hugged each other more tightly than we ever did before. Momma winced in pain. "Easy. Easy, Baby Girl, this hole in my shoulder still hurts something awful." Momma held me with her right arm as she stared caringly at Bo Daddy. Bo Daddy slowly walked to where me and Momma were embraced. She looked up at him.

"I hope she hasn't been too much trouble for you, Bo Daddy."

He smiled slyly. "Nah, not at all, gal. She be da perfect little lady, like her mudda for ole Bo Daddy. I've gotta tell ya dat ya scare da bejesus outta we both."

I stopped hugging momma and looked into her face. "Momma, I was so scared that you wouldn't wake up!" She ignored me, as she continued to stare at Bo Daddy strangely.

Bo Daddy noticed too, and tried to avoid her gaze by looking around the room. He finally worked up enough courage to look directly back at her.

"Baby?" Momma quipped.

I answered quickly, "Ma'am?"

"Why don't you go find momma some food... I'm starving."

"I sure will! I'll go see if I can find you some fish." I said excitedly.

"That sounds delicious baby, hurry up now." Smiling ear to ear, I turned to Bo Daddy.

"Come on, Bo Daddy." Momma turned her

head sharply.

"Little girl, you don't need his help for that, now git!" Puzzled, I shrugged my shoulders, and quickly ran out to find momma some food.

Nancy slid her feet and legs off the table in the direction of Bo Daddy. Looking at him sultrily as she did so. "You know, a funny thing happened when I was unconscious." Bo Daddy nervously responded. "Oh yeah, what dat be?" "I could hear everything people were saying around me. It was like being outside of my body, or something. It's kind of hard to explain, but, you know what, Mr. Bo Daddy?" "What?" He said like a little boy who already knew the answer to a question before it was asked. Nancy smiled coyly. "I heard every... single.... word.... you whispered into my ear." Bo Daddy was embarrassed and surprised. "Ya did?"

Nancy stood, and allowed the cloth covering her naked body to fall to the floor. His eyes followed the cloth all the way down to the floor. He took a deep breath and raised his head slowly. Bo Daddy saw her feet. Then, lifted his head a little higher, and saw her perfectly toned legs. Lifting his head a little more, he saw her chiseled abdominals, and ample breasts. He gulped hard, then walked closer to Nancy. He grabbed the sides of her face with his hands, and gently pulled her face to his; kissing her passionately. Their tongues united in a wild and hot-blooded dance.

Nancy pulled his jacket off violently, revealing his custom knife harness. He lifted Nancy back onto the table. She hungrily kissed him on his neck, as he unbuckled his knife harness. He lifted his arms out of it, and the harness fell to the floor with a loud thud. He once again started kissing her, as she attempted to unbutton his shirt.

Nancy successfully unbuttoned the two top buttons but unwilling to wait any longer, Bo just ripped the front of his shirt open. The rest of his buttons fell to the floor sounding like marbles as they rolled around. He flipped his shirt off, with some assistance from Nancy.

She paused and studied his pulsating pectoral muscles as they flexed up and down when he removed his shirt. She marveled at his dark brown, glossy, smooth skin-- gliding her fingertips across it. Nancy buried her face in his chest. She kissed and licked his nipples, starting on his left side slowly working her way to his right.

Bo Daddy grunted and moaned in approval, simultaneously unfastening his pants. He allowed his pants to fall to the floor and stared deeply into Nancy's eyes. She continued to kiss his chest hungrily. Bo Daddy grabbed and yanked Nancy's hair with his left hand, snapping her head back, while at the same time grabbing her buttocks firmly with his right hand, pulling her lower body sharply to the very edge of the table.

Nancy panted and moaned with anticipation. Bo Daddy bent slightly at the knees and lowered himself. He rubbed the large head of his penis up and down the already hot and moist lips of her womanhood, sending waves of ecstasy through her entire body. She convulsed and moaned, already near climax.

Without warning, Bo Daddy thrusts his hips forward, ramming his long, thick manhood into her. Nancy gasped and shrieked uncontrollably, somewhere between pain and pleasure. As he slowly worked his manhood in and out of her, she began to get used to his size, and the pain began to subside. Only pleasure remained, as she wrapped her arms around the back of his neck. Her powerful legs, she wrapped around the top of his muscular gyrating buttocks, and lifted herself off the table onto him. She timed his thrusts and began to meet him in the middle of them. Bo Daddy grunted like a wild beast in approval as they both moved together as one; she lowering herself onto him and he pumping upward into her savagely and deep.

He let go of Nancy's hair with his left hand and placed it on the other side of her waist. He began to lift her body slightly with both hands and slam her down onto his manhood. Nancy moaned, and breathed heavily. She and Bo Daddy were sweating profusely in the heat of the Kunda. Both of them were near climax, as they kissed again passionately.

Bo Daddy could no longer hold it. He began to slam Nancy down onto his manhood even more violently than before. Nancy began to climax as well, slamming herself down onto his manhood more violently, and rapidly as well.

They both simultaneously screamed and yelled in complete, unbridled ecstasy, as they climaxed in unison.

Exhausted, they fell onto the table, their bodies completely covered in sweat. They looked into each other's eyes and laughed out loud. They kissed again then embraced tenderly.

I ran back to the Kunda with some fish I had gotten from the Geechee woman Bo Daddy had charmed earlier that morning. She was even kind enough to fry them up. There are few smells that rivaled fish fried in animal fat. I ran into the Kunda and nearly dropped the plate of fish on the floor, when I saw momma and Bo Daddy laughing naked on the table. At first, I was upset, and started to barge in on the two of them. But as I backed out of the Kunda quietly, I realized, that this was the first time I had heard my momma laughing and enjoying herself-- EVER. Coming to that realization, actually made me very happy for her. Besides, I had all of that delicious fish to my greedy little self.

CHAPTER 20

Second Chance

By now, the entire Geechee enclave had heard that "Black Nancy" was alive and well, and would most likely survive her wounds. The day momma was well enough to leave the Kunda under her own strength, was a joyous occasion. I had almost forgotten momma was unconscious from the time we had arrived.

Bo Daddy, Queen Molley, and Momma, came out of the Kunda together. Momma, with her left arm in a sling, walked out and immediately squinted covering her eyes. She had been in the dark for so long, her eyes had to adjust to sunlight. She lifted her good arm to her forehead to shield her eyes, waited a few moments, and tried again. This time was not as bad. She looked around the bustling village and noticed it was full of activity.

To her right, she saw three, young Geechee girls following the instructions of a female Geechee Elder teaching them the art of weaving sweetgrass baskets. Each one of the girls sat at the knee of the Elder with their own basket on the ground in front of them-- at different stages of completion. Several yards away, she noticed at least half a dozen Geechee boys practicing their hunting skills by throwing fishing spears at a large, sweetgrass basket hanging from a tree. Further in the distance she saw many Geechee women working in the rice fields planting and cultivating, happily chanting a Geechee Shout song as they toiled.

Momma scanned the entire enclave. She watched as the thick, white smoke bellowed into the air from the chimneys of multiple huts. She took a deep breath, inhaling a mixture of unfamiliar foods cooking and fresh, salty sea air. She turned to Queen Molley, smiled and humbly said, "I have never seen such a beautiful place in this godforsaken country, Queen Molley. This is truly a blessing. I owe you my life." "Dis place be a special one, and I have done nothin'. Da ancestors saw fit to spare ya life, so da question become... 'what ya gonna do wit ya second chance?' ", Queen Molley softly replied.

Momma thought for a second, then looked at Bo Daddy. "If I were a different person, in a different time, me and my baby would stay here for the rest of our days; not worrying about anything but how many fish we could catch on a daily basis." Momma grinned, then her face slowly changed to an evil scowl. "But, it is not a different time, and I will always be who I am. The white man made me what I am now and I plan to give him heavy doses of me, every chance I get!"

Bo Daddy's facial expression changed from pleasant to troubled in an instant. He walked down the steps and walked away from the Kunda. Queen Molley followed Bo Daddy with her eyes. She reached into the front of her dress and pulled a corncob pipe from between her breasts. She placed it into her mouth, struck a matchstick on the rail in front of the Kunda, and lit her pipe. Shaking the match out with her right hand, she looked over at momma again, as she puffed her pipe and said, "Ya know, if ya chose a different path den da way of vengeance, there would be a place for ya ere wit us. We ave long wanted to ave a teacher-woman. We youngins and many a da grown folks must learn to read, and ya can be da one ta teach 'em."

Momma nodded her head and thought for a few moments once more. She turned to Queen Molley and asked, "Queen, I gotta know, this has been puzzling me since I woke up. Why do the crackers not bother you Geechees in this village?" Queen Molley gently took momma's arm and walked with her down the steps. They walked through the enclave side-by-side.

"De Bukruh do not bother we cause we are the cultivators of Carolina Gold.

"Carolina Gold? What's that?" Momma questioned, as she stopped walking and looked at Queen Molley puzzled. Queen Molley smiled and began to explain.

"Carolina Gold, be da rice, Baby. We be da only people round dese parts who know how to grow rice on dis sand patch. Dis be da number one crop in da Carolinas. Da Bukruh hate us... but, dem love da money, more dem dey hate we, ya see?"

Momma nodded once more as she began

to understand the Geechee's situation. "I'm sorry, you said the 'Bukruh'. What are the Bukruh?" Momma asked. Queen Molly giggled and placed her right hand gently onto momma's shoulder. "Why da Bukruh is da white folks, Child." Momma felt a little embarrassed. She and Queen Molley chuckled as they continued their walk through the rest of the enclave. The two of them came to a stop at the blacksmith's hut.

The blacksmith was banging away on a piece of metal. He paused his hammer when he realized Momma and Queen Molley were standing outside watching him work. He was covered in thick beads of sweat. He lowered his hammer and bowed his head respectfully towards Queen Molley. She acknowledged him by a subtle nodding of her head. Momma walked into his hut and put her hand out to shake. The blacksmith ignored momma's hand and turned his attention back to hammering on the metal.

When Queen Molley saw the blacksmith being rude to momma, she entered the hut, and walked over to him. "Bilali! Ya will stop dat blasted ammerin' now and show dis woman the 'spect she deserves—actin' like ya no ome trainin!" Queen Molley snapped angrily.

Bilali stopped hammering immediately. He put the hammer down on a table next to his anvil, wiped his right hand on his pants and shook momma's hand. "It be nice to make ya acquaintance, Ma'am," he said in his deep, raspy voice, as gently as he could muster. Queen Molley and Momma looked at one another, then Queen Molley winked at Momma.

"I have some work for you." Momma smirked and turned her back to Bilali.

"If you are willing to take it."

"What kinda work would dat be, Ma'am?" Bilali said, trying not to sound too interested. Momma walked around his hut a bit, inspecting his various tools and some of the pieces he had already shaped.

"My weapons were lost and I need you to make me some new ones."

At that moment, Queen Molley walked around Bilali's worktable and placed her arm around him like a mother in church. "Bilali be da best Blacksmith round dese parts. Even da Bukruh come to him when dey be needin' somethin' made. If ya draw it for him, ya have it in a few days. Ain't dat right?" Queen Molley suggested, as she gave him a stern look. She patted Bilali on the back. He nodded his head in agreement, hesitantly.

"Very good. I will draw it up this evening and bring it back to you." Momma said confidently.

"Dat be fine, Ma'am."

Momma and Queen Molley both made their way to the front entrance and departed-- smirking at one another as they did so. Bilali watched as they left and once they were gone, he picked his hammer back up and threw it angrily to the ground.

As they walked together back toward the Kunda, Momma spoke, "Your blacksmith doesn't appreciate me being here one bit, does he?" Queen Molley thought to herself, trying to find the most tactful way to answer. "Honestly... No, he don't. He lost one very dear to him, long ago. He feel dat you and his brudda will bring de billage trouble again."

Momma turned to Queen Molley a little insulted. "I have no intention of bringing trouble to this wonderful place. Wait, did you say brother? You mean Bo Daddy and Bilali... are brothers?" Queen Molley giggled before she answered. "Yes, dey be bruddas and da two a dem couldn't be any different then if dey came from different muddas."

It was then, Timothy and I walked up to Queen Molley and Momma in the center of the enclave. They were in the middle of what looked like a serious conversation about something. They stopped talking abruptly as they saw us approaching. Momma turned in our direction, wearing a guilty smile. "Hey baby, I see you found yourself a friend."

I blushed uncontrollably and stuttered, "Yes, I did. This is my friend Timothy. Timothy this is my momma, Miss Nancy." Timothy shyly shook momma's hand.

"It sure be a pleasure to make ya acquaintance, Ma'am."

Momma smiled at him as he shook her hand excitedly. "It's nice to meet you as well, Timothy."

Momma turned to Queen Molley smiling, "How long was I out? It seems I've missed a whole lot." Momma and Queen Molley chuckled together. Never feeling as embarrassed as I felt at that moment, I rolled my eyes and attempted to get momma to stop teasing. "Momma!"

She must have gotten the message because she immediately stopped chuckling, and got more serious as she turned to Timothy and I.

"And, where are you two going?"

She questioned. I was shocked a little by the directness of her question. Queen Molley sensing the tenseness of the moment, made her escape. "I'll be in the Kunda if ya need anyting." She smiled at us, then turned and walked toward the Kunda. I knew chances were very slim that momma would let me out of her sight, let alone go to some fishing hole with some Geechee boy she had met less than thirty seconds ago. I thought to myself and said 'here goes nothing'.

"Well, Momma, I am glad you asked that question. Timothy wants to take me to the fishing hole to swim. Can I go? Oh, please Momma!" I clasped my hands in front of Momma's face and begged. She pondered the question, as she gave Timothy the do-not-make-me-have-to-put-my-hands-on-you look.

"Mr. Timothy...?" asked Momma. Timothy

answered nervously, shaking like a leaf.

"Yes, Ma'am?" Momma walked up to Timothy until there was maybe one foot between them. She looked deep into his eyes as she raised her right hand and pointer finger.

"If one... and I mean just one, of my baby's hairs on her head is missing, I suggest you find another place to live. Do you understand?"

Timothy nodded his head rapidly and nervously. I could not believe it. I smiled uncontrollably as I ran over to Momma and kissed her excitedly and repeatedly on the cheek. "Thank you! Thank you! Thank you, Momma!"

Without any more hesitation, Timothy and I ran as fast as we could toward the woods. Momma watched as the two of us smiled at each other as we ran, disappearing into the woods. Momma yelled, "Ruby! You make sure you get back her before dark, you here!" She laughed to herself, shaking her head as she walked back toward the Kunda.

CHAPTER 21

I Can't Wait!

Timothy and I walked through the woods side-by-side, down a thin game trail. All I could hear were the sounds of birds chirping and singing, echoing throughout the thick canopy of trees. I felt a different kind of alive because momma and I never had enough time to really appreciate these kinds of things. This place was so beautiful. I looked up and saw an Oak Tree, its massive branches hung over the game trail covered with long beards of Spanish Moss; the wind gently blew, moving its leaves and branches back and forth, allowing bits of sunlight to pierce the dense foliage of the canopy. Timothy watched me as I lost myself in the beauty.

He reached out gently and took my hand. The two of us continued down the game trail hand-in-hand, when suddenly, we both heard the unnatural rustling of leaves. We stopped immediately and surveyed the surrounding bushes. Timothy tensed and turned his head slightly, while scanning our surroundings. "Did ya eer dat?" I stood motionless, and got low, as momma had conditioned me to do. "Yeah, I heard it."

I whispered, while concentrating on what I thought were prime ambush locations around us. Timothy, trying to keep the in-control-male role, offered up his assessment. "It be da wind probably...or some cridda." I decided not to burst his bubble, and allowed him to take the lead. Besides, he was the first boy to ever show any interest. I did not want to scare him away by being RUBY–WARRIOR GIRL, or something like that.

Timothy squeezed my hand tighter, and then led me down the game trail once more. We meandered cautiously along the trail until we came to another large Oak. Suddenly, I heard four sets of feet scurry across the game trail behind us. Timothy and I spun around, and looked, but saw nothing. I signaled to him silently, by moving my head, that we should continue walking. Timothy nodded, and we took a few steps, then, turned around quickly once more in unison. We saw four figures caught out in the open. They attempted to jump off the trail and into the woods, but it was too late. Timothy bravely yelled out, "I see ya! Ya can show yaselves!"

We were both confused. I turned to Timothy, with my heart racing, trying to keep myself under control. "Do you know who it is?" We heard the sound of twigs breaking underfoot. The four dark figures came into view. I sighed in relief, when I saw that it was only four Geechee youth from the enclave-- three boys and a girl. "What da ell are ya doin following me?" Timothy snapped, obviously annoyed.

The smallest of the four, a boy, who was standing in front of the others, walked toward Timothy defiantly and said "We want to go to da fishin hole... to swim." The other three nodded their heads frantically at Timothy.

Timothy, who had planned for us two to be alone at the hole, scowled angrily at them all. "Why, ya gotta pick today, of all days!" he bemoaned, not doing a good job of hiding his disappointment. The little boy answered quick and decisive. "We pick today, cause it be damn hot out ere!"

The little boy lifted his arm into the air, like a general leading his troops, and signaled the others to move forward. They all smirked at Timothy as they mockingly marched past him, on their way to the fishing hole. Timothy clinched his fist angrily, as he watched the teens walk down the trail.

I held my laughter in for as long as I could, but burst out laughing uncontrollably as I turned to Timothy and teased, "What's wrong? You mad, cause you were trying to have me out here in these woods all to yourself, huh? Shame on you! Shame, shame, shame!" I chuckled as I started down the trail again. Timothy threw up his hands in humiliation and frustration, as he started down the trail again as well.

We finally reached the end of the game trail but were now facing a very steep hill. He climbed it first, then like a real gentleman turned and extended his hand out to me. I took his hand in the fashion I had seen the white ladies do whenever they were being helped out of carriages, and such, by white gentlemen. Timothy helped me up the hill. Once at the top, he and I looked down into the clearest freshwater fishing hole I think I have ever seen.

The other teens from the enclave were already in the water, splashing, jumping and swimming around. Timothy and I looked at one another and without warning, each of us bolted for the water down the hill. I stood on the bank watching the teens frolic and splash one another. I remember thinking I had never seen black children playing so freely, as if they hadn't a care in this world. It was great!

Timothy sat on the ground at waters' end to remove his shoes. He pulled the left, then the right one off and jumped to his feet. He backed away from the water to get a running start. Timothy sprinted toward the water without hesitation and jumped as high and long as he could, splashing the teens with a wave of water in the process. They loved it! I laughed hysterically, as did the teens. I looked up and noticed the thick branch of a tree on the bank of the fishing hole hanging over the water, which gave me an idea.

I made my way over to the bank, walked over to the tree and began to climb. Timothy and the others watched in awe as I climbed out onto the limb, stood and carefully balanced myself with both my arms extended out to my sides. Once in the center of the branch I gathered myself, and leaped backward, flipping into the water, remaining underwater for a long time.

Timothy and the others waited for me to surface. When I did not, they all became concerned. Timothy quickly moved through the water trying to find where I was. The teens followed suit, calling out to me, and moving through the water as well to the spot in which I had landed. Suddenly, I sprung from beneath the water and scared the hell out of all of them! They jumped nearly out of their skins, which was my intention all along. I laughed loudly, as I splashed them rapidly. They laughed and began to splash me as well.

Unbeknownst to us, Bishop and his men were riding nearby and heard the youthful sounds of splashing and laughing. He turned to his men and whispered, "Let's check this out.

Dismount." He and his men dismounted their horses and tied them off to some of the surrounding bushes. They began to creep their way through the woods toward the sound of our happy voices.

Bishop came to the small rise at the top of the fishing hole. He signaled his men to surround the hole. He belly-crawled up to the lip of the rise and peeked down. Unfortunately, we were oblivious to the strangers spying on us, completely lost in youthful frivolity; something I had never experienced.

Bishop studied each face of the teens in the fishing hole. That's when he saw me, and his eyes lit up. He pulled his pistol from its holster and stood, yelling down into the hole.

"Well! Well! Well! What do we have here?"

Startled, we stopped immediately and turned toward the direction of the voice. When I saw whom the voice belonged, my heart sank and I felt like I had to use the outhouse. I thought my eyes were playing tricks on me; hoping they were playing tricks on me.

Timothy and the others were confused and afraid as well. The four teens from the enclave quickly made their way to the bank opposite Bishop. They attempted to run up the hill but just before they reached the top, three of Bishop's men stood up from their hiding places and drew down on the fleeing teens with muskets and pistols.

They stopped instantly, raised their hands and began to slowly back down the hill. Bishop's men, with guns trained on them, slowly made their way down the hill as well. The rest of Bishop's men stood up from their hiding places and came down to the water's edge.

Timothy and I slowly made our way out of the water to where the teens were standing on the bank. My heart was beating fast as I scanned the tops of the hills surrounding the fishing hole, praying that behind one of the trees or rocks or anything, my momma was watching; preparing to come and save me, like she always done.

But instead, Bishop came down the hill with that disgusting smirk he always wore on that scarred face of his. "I want you all in a straight line." He said smugly.

Bishop's men began to push and pull us into a straight line, with all of our backs to the water. As he walked in front of us, he stared into each of our faces as he passed. Bishop stopped when he got in front of me. Playfully he spoke, "I know you, don't I?"

I was trembling uncontrollably. I closed my eyes and began to get flashes from the past; memories I had, until that moment, forgotten.

I remembered me as a little girl being lead by Bishop down a hallway at the old plantation. I remembered him taking me into one of the rooms in the "Society's" hotel. I remembered him ripping my tiny clothes off, and throwing me onto the bed. I remembered him jumping on top of me holding my tiny arms down over my head and covering my mouth. I also remembered a sharp pain in my privates before momma kicked in the door and sliced Bishop's face with her sickle.

At that moment, I summoned all of my courage and opened my eyes. "No sir, I'se neva seen ya before ins me life." Bishop placed his pistol back into its holster and began to applaud. "That was a very good attempt at Geechee...but you and I both know that your momma would not approve of you speaking so improperly...

Ruby." My heart sank, as he asked me forcefully, "Where is your momma?"

Realizing my play-acting had not worked, I answered.

"You're too late. My momma died of a bullet wound she got from you at Miss Abbey's place." Bishop looked at me and snickered.

"I knew that I winged the ole girl out there! So you're sayin' that your momma, Black Nancy, is dead. Is that right?"

"Yes, that's what I'm telling you. Please let these others go. It's me you want. They have nothing to do with it."

Bishop began to walk down the line of us, scratching his head under his hat. He stopped in front of the teen girl, who was weeping uncontrollably, gripped with fear. Bishop stared at her and asked, "So... the infamous Black Nancy is dead, huh?"

He turned toward me, and smiled, then pulled his pistol and placed the barrel between the eyes of the teen girl. He pulled the trigger and shot her without even a thought. The impact of the minie ball lifted her body backwards into the air and into the fishing hole. The remaining teens panicked. They scattered, and attempted to escape up the steep hills surrounding the hole.

One of Bishop's men raised his rifle and took aim on the short little boy, who was scratching and clawing desperately up the hill. He fired and shot the boy in his back. The boy screamed out for his momma when he was hit. His eyes widened as he reached toward the sky and fell backwards, rolling back down the hill.

The two other teens faired no better. Bishop's men quickly fired in unison, hitting them multiple times. Their bodies shook with each impact of lead striking their young bodies. Bishop reloaded his pistol then walked over to Timothy and placed its hot barrel to his forehead. I stood their helpless, still trembling and crying. "No! Please don't hurt him!" I yelled from desperation. Bishop ignored my pleas, as he asked his question more seriously. "Tell me where your momma is before I blow this nigga's fucking head off his shoulders!"

All I knew at that moment was I did not want to loose the closest thing to a relationship I had ever known. This weakened me to the point where I was prepared to do anything to save him.

"Okay, okay, I'll tell you. Just don't hurt him, please!" I looked over at Timothy as I was about to speak. He shook his head emphatically 'NO!'. I turned my head away. "I'm sorry, I have to..." Then blurted out, "Momma is not dead!" I broke down.

Bishop smiled widely at me, then, turned to his men. "You see, boys, I knew ole Nancy wasn't dead!" Bishop's men laughed loudly. "Damn boy, you must of made a hell of an impression on my little gal. Now where is she?"

I raised my head at Timothy once more. He looked back at me disappointed I had given the Bukruh information of my mother's status.

"My momma is..." Timothy interrupted, yelling to me

"Goodbye, Ruby!"

He quickly grabbed Bishop's hand with the pistol in it, placed his own thumb on the trigger, and pressed. Bishop's pistol discharged with a loud bang and white smoke wafted from its barrel into the air. Timothy's head rocked back and a blank look came over his face. His body turned slightly in my direction, and he looked directly at me, revealing a perfectly circular minie ball wound, in the center of his forehead. Blood trickled from the wound as he fell limply to the ground.

I screamed, and ran over to his lifeless body, kneeled beside him, and rubbed his face with my hands. Bishop stood there in shock and disbelief of the conviction he had just witnessed. He backed away, pulling a hanky from his pants pocket to wipe Timothy's blood from his face. He continued to stare at Timothy's body. Then, tried to regain his composure by asking me the same question. "You were about to say where your momma is?"

I ignored him and kissed my Timothy on his right cheek softly, whispering 'goodbye' and 'I love you' into his ear. With my back to Bishop and his men, I slowly stood and turned to face them all. Strangely, the fear I had once felt was now replaced by rage. I looked into each of their individual faces defiantly.

"I... can't... wait..." were the only words that came out of my mouth.

Bishop and his men turned and looked at one another quizzically. Bishop laughed and turned his head back into my direction.

"You can't wait? Can't wait for what?" He said nonchalantly. I took a deep breath before I answered.

"I can't wait for my momma to see what you did here today... so she can come and wipe you crackas out!"

Bishop laughed again, but this time it was a wicked laugh. "That's exactly what I want her to do, little lady." He walked toward me, and slowly began to loosen his belt buckle. I looked around desperately trying to find an opening for escape.

Suddenly, all of his men began to close the circle tightly around me. Two of them grabbed me by the arms and took me to the ground. I struggled as much as I could, but they were just too strong for me to break free. Bishop climbed on top of me and licked my face from my chin to my forehead. My skin crawled and the food I had eaten that morning made its way to my throat. His men laughed, jeered, and snickered, as he reached under my dress, snatching my undergarments off.

I looked into his cold black eyes, hoping to appeal to whatever small portion of humanity he had left in him. "Please don't do this! Please... please, don't do this!"

Bishop just smiled widely, brushing my hair out of my face. "There now, gal, hush yourself. Now you know I never got to finish what I started all those years ago. Your momma's not here to interrupt me this time, is she? I've been thinking for a long time, that I'm tired of chasing her. It's time she come lookin' for me!"

Bishop's smile slowly became a scowl as he forced my legs apart with his legs and in one swift move, penetrated me. All I truly remember is letting out the most piercing scream in my life and as I looked up into the sky. The birds in the surrounding trees took flight overhead as if they didn't want to witness what was about to happen.

One by one, they took my innocence, over, and over again. They violated me in ways I could never have imagined on my own. Bishop and his men had vanished as quickly as they had appeared. When I finally came to I was completely naked and alone. The pain in my private areas was nearly unbearable and my eyes were nearly shut from swelling, after some of Bishop's men beat and slapped me around, as they had their way.

I used the rage and hatred I felt inside to help me struggle to my feet. I found my torn dress and tried to cover my body. Then I limped down the hill toward the game trail and prayed I was going in the right direction-- toward the enclave.

Blood dripped from my womanhood as I struggled to walk. My head hurt and I couldn't see very well. I ached all over and every sound in the woods startled me. I don't really know how long it took me to get back to the enclave, or even how. I do remember being ready to lay down and give up. I slouched down beside a large pine tree and began to cry. All I could hear in my head was momma preaching to me, "Never give up! Once that happens, you're as good as dead."

I had almost completely given up. Then, I felt it-- a stiff, cool breeze, carrying the fresh smell of salt on it. I knew I had to be close to the shore. On the following breeze, I heard the sounds of Ring Shouters in the distance, and people double-clapping their hands in unison. I knew it had to be the enclave. A new strength had come over me. I leapt to my feet and began tearing and fighting my way through the thick brush on the other side of the pine tree.

Once through, I felt the cool sand under my bare, tired feet. Squinting, I held my head back to achieve the best angle to see. My heart pounded feverishly when I saw the Kunda, with every lamp inside illuminating from the windows. The Ring Shout was at a fever pitch. I stumbled, crawled, and clawed my way to the large doors of the Kunda.

The entire village was inside watching a group of Ring Shouters. Peeking through a side window, I searched for momma or Bo Daddy. Finally, I spotted them seated in the front row. They were enjoying themselves, smiling and clapping to the music. Queen Molley was seated next to Bilali, also enjoying the performance. Everyone was clapping their hands and stamping their feet. I saw the Conjurer jump to her feet and began dancing with the performers like she was a young woman again.

I made my way to the doors and pushed

with the last bit of strength I could muster. The doors swung open and I hobbled through the threshold, battered and bloodied, my clothes tattered. At first, no one noticed my condition but once I got to the center of the aisle, a woman seated to my left saw my condition, and screamed at the top of her lungs. "Oh Lawd have mercy!"

The Ring Shouters stopped mid-song and stood perplexed staring at me. Momma looked on puzzled, as the Ring Shouters started to stand and stare. She turned in her chair and saw me. Momma leapt from where she was sitting, to where I was. I reached out for her with my right hand, collapsing into her arms exhausted. "Momma they, they..." I lost consciousness.

Momma pulled me close to her breast and held me tightly with tears rolling down her cheeks. "I know baby... I know what those crackas did!" Bo Daddy ran over to momma. He knelt down and picked me up into his arms gently. Bilali glared at Bo Daddy as he and momma passed him on the way outside.

Timothy's mother watched as Bo Daddy carried me out. She scanned the room and when she realized that Timothy had not returned with me, she let out a deafening shriek, and in a mother's agony, fell to the floor. The other women seated around her came to her aid immediately.

Bilali followed Bo Daddy and momma outside and yelled for all to hear. "Are ya appy now, brudda? I tole ya dat death and destruction follow ya, where eva ya are!" Bo Daddy could not keep his anger in check any longer. He handed me to momma and started walking quickly toward Bilali. Bilali defiantly walked down the steps of the Kunda to meet Bo Daddy.

Momma knew that Bo Daddy intended to kill his brother, right then. "Bo Daddy! We ain't got time for this. We gotta take care of my baby, now!" Bo Daddy, much to everyone's surprise, stopped dead in his tracks. He scowled menacingly at Bilali, then, turned around and walked back to where momma was waiting on him.

Bilali continued to badger Bo Daddy as he and momma quickly made their way to a hut where they could tend to my wounds. "I tole ya dis would appen!" Bilali spat on the ground angrily as he walked back into the Kunda. The villagers began murmuring loudly about all that had just transpired.

Bo Daddy entered the hut behind momma. He struck a match and lit a torch that was hanging on the wall. Momma quickly brought me to the makeshift bed and laid me down. She carefully inspected my injuries in the light. Both my eyes were swollen shut, both nostrils were bleeding, my lips were busted, and grotesquely swollen as well.

Once momma saw the extent of the injuries, she found it impossible to keep her emotions under control. I awoke long enough to get a few words out. "Momma, I hurt all over." I moanded. She kissed me on the forehead, like she always did. "I know, baby. Hush now. Try not to move too much. You just rest now." Bo Daddy was standing next to the torch, seething-- watching me and momma. Momma turned her head slightly towards him.

"Bo Daddy? I need you to get me some water, so I can clean my baby up. Please." Momma broke down sobbing. She pulled me to her again and held me tight. Bo Daddy ran out of the hut to get water. Momma looked down into my eyes with a look I have seen for as long as I can remember. Momma was gonna kill them crackas and I knew it. I swallowed deeply, tasting my own blood, then whispered to her. "Momma, you can't go after Bishop. That's what he wants you to do. That's why he did this to me-- he wants you to come after him. He all but told me so."

I must have strained too much because I passed out again in momma's arms. She laid me down on the bed once more. Just then, Bo Daddy returned out of breath with a bucket of water, and quickly placed it next to momma. She looked up at Bo Daddy helplessly crying, "Look what dem crackas did to my baby, Bo Daddy! Look what they did!"

He slowly lowered himself to the floor next to momma, reached his arms around her, and held her as tightly as he could.

CHAPTER 22

The Promise

Bilali, in deep thought, came out of the Kunda staring at the hut where I lay. He walked to his work hut and entered, lighting the torch inside. Then went to the furnace and stoked the flames, pressing the handle of a large air bellow with his feet. From the corner of his eye he saw something lying on his worktable. It was a large piece of paper with an intricate, hand-drawn design on it. Bilali lifted the paper and studied the drawing. He walked over to the wall nearest his work area and hung it.

Turning to his metal storage area, he selected a large piece of steel and placed it into the red-hot furnace. After giving the metal time to heat, with large steel pincers, he removed the glowing red-hot piece of metal from the furnace, carefully laying it onto his anvil. The visibly perturbed blacksmith removed the large steel hammer from the tool wall and began to beat the piece of steel. Sparks flew into the air each time he struck it with his hammer.

Meanwhile, outside, The Conjurer led a procession through the middle of the enclave. Queen Molley walked behind the Conjurer, followed by the mothers and fathers of the children who were killed by Bishop and his men. Men from the enclave were pulling the children's bodies in a single file line. Shrouded in black, each child was in their own individual cart. The Geechee villagers chanted somberly.

Momma and Bo Daddy heard the villagers chanting, so they went outside of the hut to see the procession and to pay their respects. Momma and Bo Daddy hung their heads, as the mother's of the dead children turned and stared at them with blame in their faces, as they passed. Momma ashamed turned to Bo Daddy. "This is all my fault, Bo."

Bo Daddy tried to comfort momma and placed his arm around her.

"Dis is not ya fault. Ya didn't know where I was taken ya. I had to bring ya eer to save ya life, gal."

Momma looked up at him annoyed. "Is that supposed to make me feel better, or something?"

Momma turned the rest of her body around and took Bo Daddy's hands into hers. Looking into his eyes she said softly,

"Bo Daddy, I want you to promise me something." He looked into momma's eyes suspiciously.

"Anyting."

Momma gripped his hands tightly.

"If something happens to me, I want you to swear that you'll get my Ruby up North. I don't ever want her to have to live like me... like an animal."

Bo Daddy grabbed momma with both arms and pulled her to him.

"Dis not be your fault, Nancy! Dis be dat Bukruh, dat Bishop fault. So ya don't blame yaself, da ya eer me, gal!"

Bo Daddy studied momma, then backed away a little. He realized his pleas had just fallen on deaf ears.

"Just swear that you'll do as I ask."

Dejectedly, he lowered his head and sighed.

"Okay, me swear, me swear. But, me have one question for ya." Bo Daddy gently brushed momma's hair away from her face.

"What's the question, Bo?" He looked into momma's eyes with all the sincerity he possessed.

"What makes ya tink, that I would ever let you go anywhere witout me?"

Stunned, momma pulled away from Bo Daddy and turned her back to him angrily.

"Bo Daddy, don't make this harder than it already is for me. This is not your fight!"

Bo Daddy, agitated, grabbed momma's shoulder and spun her around to face him once more. "Not me fight! Ave ya lost ya mind, gal? If me memba correctly, it be Bo Daddy who cut da troat of da Bukruh tryin to git ya friend Missy in da woods, was it not? It be da Bo Daddy who get dem horses, for we to escape dis Bishop at ole Miss Abbey's, and it sure be da Bo Daddy who stick the Bukruh spy in da woods a few days back!"

Momma was shocked. She hugged him tightly. "I'm so sorry, Bo. You have been there for us, and I thank you. But, what I do now, I do to protect this village and the people in it. The most important thing is that, in this horrible time of slavery, these people are a shining example of what our people can accomplish when given a chance. I've never seen such a self-sufficient black community in this hellish land until I came to this place. I swear on the soul of my child, that not a thousand Bishops are gonna terrorize this place... not while I draw breath!" Momma turned and walked back into the hut. Bo Daddy followed.

CHAPTER 23

A Godsend

In the town of Savannah, the Sheriff slammed his fist on his desk and yelled. "You did what!? Are you outta your fuckin mind?" Bishop calmly sat in a wooden chair in front of the Sheriff's desk cleaning his nails with the tip of his knife. Sheriff Parker continued to berate him.

"Son, do you know what's at stake here? Well, let me shed some fuckin light on it for ya. We have not had one, I mean one, fuckin problem outta dem Geechees, in a hundred fuckin years! You ain't been in my county for a fuckin week, and you killed four of em? Are you fuckin kidden me?"

Bishop laughed disrespectfully, then, smugly rebutted. "Sheriff, I fail to see what the big deal is. Those niggers attacked me, and my men, and we were forced to defend ourselves. Sheriff, you should know how unpredictable niggers can be."

Sheriff Parker was beside himself. He walked over to the large picture window in the front of his office and placed his hands behind his back. "Unpredictable huh? Well, Mr. Bishop, I'll tell you one thing I predict. I predict, that right now, while we're talking about this, Queen Molley is thinking of fifty ways to cut your fucking balls off. The funny thing is, I have a good mind to let her."

"What do you mean?" Bishop said, as he looked at Sheriff Parker puzzled. The Sheriff walked around his desk and took a seat. He reached out for the large bowl of peanuts, which sat in the center of his desk. Removing one, he cracked it open and tossed the nuts into his mouth, then threw the shells onto the floor. He sat back in his chair and looked at Bishop. "I mean it would probably be easier if I would just let the Geechees have you, that's all." Sheriff Parker shot Bishop a sly smirk.

Bishop, offended by the Sheriff's comments, stood abruptly. "Sir! You call yourself a Southerner!" Sheriff Parker lifted his right hand into the air slightly and pointed his finger to the floor, motioning Bishop to sit. "No sir, I do not. I call myself a businessman. Those niggers, as you like to call them, are the only farmers in this entire state, who know how to cultivate this states' number one, that's right, number one crop... RICE! Those Geechees are worth their weight in gold, son. What are you worth?"

Bishop, insulted further, jumped from his chair and quickly walked to the front door of the office. Sheriff Parker stood. "Mr. Bishop! I did not say I wouldn't help you." Bishop smirked and turned slowly toward the Sheriff. "Finally, some good news." Sheriff Parker sat back in his chair and calmly grabbed another peanut, cracked it, and tossed the seed into his mouth. "You'll find the kind of men you'll be needin' in the saloon up the street... but it's gonna cost ya. Them boys don't come cheap, but they're pretty reliable, if you know what I mean." He tipped his hat to the Sheriff and left the office.

Bishop walked into the saloon and made his way over to the bar. The bartender watched this stranger, wearing the black duster with cocked hat to match, as he cleaned a glass with a white rag. He placed the glass onto the bar and walked over to Bishop, "What'll you have, Mister?" He muttered. Bishop looked around the room, which was somewhat empty, except for four men playing poker at a table in the very back of the saloon.

Before Bishop could respond, three more men walked through the swinging doors at the entrance laughing loudly. They all walked over to the bar. One of those men, the tallest of them, slapped his hand down on top of the bar. "Bartender! Get me and my friends a bottle of whiskey!"

The bartender quickly grabbed a full bottle of whiskey from beneath the bar, placing it on the bar and sliding the bottle across it. One of the three men at the bar, a bearded man, stopped the bottle from sliding and removed the cork with his brown, rotten teeth. He reached over behind the bar and grabbed three shot glasses, which he placed in front of himself. The bearded man poured whisky into all three glasses. He passed two of the shot glasses to his friends. They raised their glasses and took the shots together.

Bishop studied the men, then, looked at the bartender. "I'll have a Brandy." "Coming right up, Sir!" The bartender responded quickly without lifting his head. He pulled a shot glass from beneath the bar and placed it in front of Bishop. The bartender turned and grabbed a bottle from a shelf, hanging on the wall behind him, then turned back around, pulled the cork from the bottle and poured Bishop a shot. Bishop grabbed the shot glass and tossed the contents to the back of his throat. He slammed the empty glass onto the bar. "I'll have another." The bartender poured him another. Bishop looked at the bartender inquisitively and asked so all could hear, "Tell me, do you know any men around here, who might be interested in making some money?"

The four men playing poker stopped when they heard the mention of money. The most unsavory looking of the bunch stood and began to walk toward Bishop. His beard had leftover bits of food in it, his skin was caked with dirt and grime and his vest had two mini ball holes on the left side. He stopped, and stood next to Bishop at the bar, turning his head slightly. "Did I hear you right, Mister? You lookin for some men?" Bishop swigged down his second shot then turned to face the dirty man, looking him up and down, scrunching his face up from the stench. "Yes, you did hear me correctly. I need more men to go after a ruthless nigger fugitive by the name of Black Nancy."

The filthy man snatched the bottle of Brandy from the bartender's hand and poured Bishop another drink. He reached behind the bar and grabbed a glass from behind it. He stared at Bishop, and chuckled as he poured a drink for himself as well. Then he introduced himself, "They call me Dirty Sam." Bishop watched the man closely as he poured the Brandy. "It seems to me that I heard of this Black Nancy before. Some say, it would be better to tongue kiss a rattlesnake, then tangle with her!" He burst into hysterical laughter and slapped Bishop on the back hard. "Well, you can count me and my boys in. Hey, how much you payin' anyway?"

Bishop swigged down the drink poured for him and announced, "Alright, Dirty Sam, I'll pay each man five dollars a day, and fifty dollars, to the man that kills the bitch! We leave in the morning. I have another nine men camped near the coast. That should be more than enough to catch her." All the other men in the bar rushed over to Bishop in celebration of their new employment. One by one, they walked up to him and shook his hand excitedly as if he were a godsend.

CHAPTER 24

On My Soul

Momma, Bo Daddy and I went to the village cemetery to pay our last respects, to Timothy, and the other children. We stood looking down at their graves, which all had small African face jugs on them. Handmade toys, and fruit for their journey to the other side, had been laid on top of each grave as well. Momma and Bo Daddy stood their silent and somber. I stood there reminiscing about what was, and what could have been between sweet Timothy and I. The picture of him saying those last words, 'Goodbye, Ruby', before sacrificing himself for me to retain what little honor I had left-- played over, and over again in my mind.

My eyes swelled with tears, as I looked at each individual tiny grave again. I pondered on what makes our races so different from one another. I turned my head and saw a beautiful bunch of wildflowers. I walked over to pick them. I could not believe it, when I counted there were only four-- one for each of the fallen. I picked them and limped back over to the graves, laying one flower on each, kissing the last, before placing it atop Timothy's grave.

Still in pain, I tried my best to ignore it, and knelt beside his grave with some assistance from momma and Bo Daddy. "You were the bravest boy I ever met, and I will miss you." I kissed my palm and placed it onto the top of his grave, and said goodbye. Momma helped me back to my feet and she, me and Bo, headed back toward the enclave. Momma placed her arm around me, lovingly, as we walked together.

We had gotten to the center of the enclave, when we were met by Queen Molley and the Conjurer.

"Miss Nancy, da people of da billage and meself, would like to ave a word wit cha if we could, in da Kunda," she said to us respectfully.

"Okay, we'll be there." I answered while wincing.

Queen Molley rebutted sternly. "No, not all of

ya. Just you, Nancy." Queen Molley and the Conjurer abruptly turned and walked toward the Kunda.

We all turned and looked at one another with concern. Momma smiled at us both. Bo Daddy looked at momma. "Do ya want me to come wit cha, Nancy?" He asked. She bent down, kissed me on the forehead, and then stood up straight. "No Bo, it'll be alright. They probably just want me to get the hell out of town sooner, rather than later." She gave Bo Daddy a half-hearted smile, then turned toward the Kunda. "Don't worry, I'll be back directly."

As momma approached the Kunda, she heard a Ring Shout going on inside. It sounded like a celebration. The sound of bongos filled the air. The melodic rhythm became more intense with each of her steps closer to the Kunda. Momma prepared herself for the worst as she climbed the steps. She took a deep breath before entering the doors. Much to her amazement, the Geechees were inside dancing joyfully. Momma walked through the threshold, looking around at everyone.

The Conjurer walked through the crowd

of villagers to momma. She took her hand into her own, and led her to the center of the room. Once there the Conjurer raised her hand and the bongo player stopped playing immediately and the dancers froze in place. All at once, the Geechees knelt and put their heads down in prayer. Momma was confused as she surveyed the room. Queen Molley stood and walked to the center of the room. She took momma's other hand into hers.

The Conjurer began to wave her hands over her head, then turned around and took the hands of Momma and Queen Molley as she attempted to conjure the spirits.

"Holy spirits of the ancestors, 'ear me now. Protect dis woman, dis vessel of vengeance. Make her faster and stronger den she were before. Make her da eye of we storm of wrath. 'Elp her strike down da demon Bukruh, who take da lives of our innocents. Ancestors of da void, 'ear me!"

Suddenly, a wind began to blow the flames of the torches. The large front doors blew open, startling those inside. The Geechees began to chant loudly. Suddenly, as quickly as it had begun, the wind stopped and the Geechees stopped chanting at the same time.

Momma's eyes were closed. She opened them and turned to Queen Molley, nodded to her, then turned to the villagers. "I thank each and every one of you, for your forgiveness, and the generosity you have shown me and my daughter. I swear on my soul, that the men responsible for the killing of your children, will pay the ultimate price, before the sun sets on this village tomorrow!" The villagers cheered and pumped their fists in the air angrily.

At that moment, Bilali entered the Kunda carrying something with both his hands. It was covered with a colorful piece of Kente cloth. Still at a fever pitch inside the Kunda, the villagers began to notice Bilali standing in the entrance. Their excitement subsided to a murmur, as all of their eyes became trained on him. Momma and Queen Molley turned their attention to Bilali as well.

He stood expressionless at the doorway, then, walked slowly through the villagers who parted, allowing him through the center of the room. He came to a stop in front of momma, who watched him suspiciously. "If ya gonna cut da Bukruh down, who done dis to our youngins...ya gonna need dese."

Bilali removed the cloth from the object he was holding and revealed a beautifully, hand-crafted pair of sickles. The sickles had protective handles, to protect the wielder's hands. At the base of the handles was an exquisite monogram of the capitol letters which read *B.N.* in old English Script. Momma's eyes lit up as she reached out to touch her newly forged weapons for the first time. She looked up into Bilali's eyes and nodded to him with respect.

Queen Molley smiled widely at momma. She walked toward her and said, "ya can't just carry them in ya hands, so one of we best leather workers made ya dis." Queen Molley pointed to an elderly woman in the crowd. She slowly made her way through the crowd with a beautiful leather harness for the sickles. It was a whole lot fancier than her old one. The woman handed it to momma. Momma took it and raised it into the air for all to see. Once again, the Geechees erupted into cheering.

CHAPTER 25

Never Forget Who You Are

The next morning momma was
up and out of the hut before the sun had risen.
The crickets were still serenading in the dark and
the cool, misty air hovered over the enclave. It
felt like rain was coming. I limped my way over
to the back window of the hut, to watch her, as
she prepared herself for battle. Momma wore a
wide leather strap across her breasts and a
leather loincloth to match. She dressed that way
so as not to restrict her movement in any way.
She was wearing her new leather harness, which
was reminiscent of her pit-fighting days.

The moon reflected off her jet-black skin,
showing a perfect outline of her tremendously
developed body. Momma did a series of left and
right swings with her new sickles. I could hear
her weapons cutting through the wind. She stood

with her feet shoulder width apart, and skillfully twirled the weapons in each hand; until her body glistened with sweat.

Bo Daddy slept next to his little sister's grave all night. When he awoke, he sat next to the grave sharpening all of his knives with a wet stone, as he sang her favorite Ring Shout song to her, *Gabriel Blow Your Trumpet*.

Bilali walked out of his blacksmith hut wearing a custom metal chest plate. The plate was an inch thick. He too practiced with his weapons of choice. Twirling a large steel hammer attached to a leather strap around his left hand, and another around his right. When he twirled his hammers, you could hear them also cut the wind. Bilali twirled, then, rested his hammers on both shoulders as he walked toward the Kunda.

Momma's eyes were closed as she swung her weapons as hard and as fast as she could. She saw in her mind's eye Samuel's face being bashed in, Missy being tortured, Daisy dying in her arms, Miss Abbey being shot, The Geechee Children gunned down, and finally me being raped and beaten by Bishop and his men.

Momma growled as she flipped the blades of her sickles backward, giving her the ability to punch her opponents with blade hand protectors. Momma punched the air with her weapons rapidly with multiple lefts and rights. She left her last punch extended, then, opened her eyes breathing very heavily.

Bo Daddy rubbed his last blade onto the wet stone as he came to the end of the Geechee song. He placed the knife into the last empty space on his knife vest, leaned over and kissed the cross on his little sister's grave. "Me tink, me be seein ya, real soon, baby gal." He stood and walked toward the enclave.

Momma walked to the front of the hut where her horse was tied. Queen Molley was waiting for her by the horse.

"You'll be leavin soon den?" Queen Molley said somberly. Momma looked into her eyes.

"I don't have the words, Queen Molley."

"There are none to be said child." Momma nodded with her head down, then, lifted it.

"About my Ruby..." Queen Molley interrupted momma.

"Ya don't ave ta worry. She memba of da

billage now. Ya need ta concentrate on what ya must do."

I came out of the hut as momma prepared to mount the horse. I limped over to her and embraced her as tightly as possible.

"I love you, momma." I whispered into her ear. Even though I have told my momma I loved her hundreds of times, somehow, this time I meant it more than any other. She looked down at me, trying to keep herself together.

"I know, baby... and momma loves you too. Never forget who you are—the granddaughter of Chief Yoruba of the Ashanti Empire... and I love you."

As tears rolled down her cheeks. She kissed me on the forehead, turned and mounted the horse. She tugged on the reins and rode off.

Queen Molley walked over and placed her arm around me, as we both watched momma ride through the village. Every Geechee in the enclave, male and female, lined the way through the village for momma, bowing their heads as she rode past. Bo Daddy suddenly walked in front of momma's horse at the edge of the village. "Now, jus where da hell, do ya tink ya goin, without da Bo Daddy?" Momma sat back in the saddle, looked around and sighed. "Bo, I have to do this by myself!" He looked up at momma annoyed. "And why is dat? Do ya tink ya da only one who has a reason to kill Bukruh? Or is it dat ya don't enjoy me company?" Momma looked down at him angrily. "No, that's not it..." "Good! Den dat's settled!" Bo Daddy interrupted confidently, as he turned and began walking quickly towards the woods. Momma sighed loudly, dug her heals into the flanks of her horse, and started riding toward the woods following behind him.

CHAPTER 26

Like A Crazed Animal

In Bishop's camp near the coast, one man kept watch, while sitting on a large rock with his musket resting between his legs. His musket was pointed straight up, as he held it with both hands resting his head on them. He struggled to stay awake as a few drops of rain began to fall. He nodded to sleep again but became frustrated and pulled the blanket over his head to protect himself from the annoying raindrops.

He heard a noise and uncovered his face, scanning the woods around him, but saw nothing. Once again, he covered his face until a twig broke, and he quickly removed the blanket from his eyes, seeing momma's muscular legs directly in front of him. He shook like a leaf, as he followed momma's legs slowly up to her angry face looking down on him.

Momma swiftly placed the blade of the sickle in her right hand beneath the man's chin, digging into his skin with the point, forcing him to stand. She leaned into his ear, whispering, "I'll ask you this one time. Where is Bishop?"

The lookout was so frightened he could not speak. Momma, a woman of her word, shoved the sickle up through the bottom of the man's chin-- her blade could be seen inside of his mouth. His eyes rolled into the back of his head as he fell to the ground.

The rain began to fall harder. Bishop's other men warmed themselves around a large campfire. They were sitting on the ground inside of a lean-to. A tall man yelled in frustration.

"Shit! Where in the hell is Bishop? That son-of-a-bitch left us out here to fuckin' drown, while he gets to go to town, with all them whores and such!"

A burly man turned to him. "Why don't you shut the hell up? Bishop will be back shortly, then we'll go destroy that niggra village over yonder; kill all the bucks and take any one of them niggra bitches you want. But not until we get Black Nancy, my friend. Not until!"

The burly man laughed, disgustingly snorting like a pig. The tall one stood and pulled the collar of his coat up onto his neck.

"Sounds good, fat man. Shit! I feel better already. I gotta drain the lizard."

He left the lean-to and walked away from the others until he came to a large tree. The tall man stood in front of the tree, spread his legs slightly and unbuttoned his fly. The man closed his eyes and leaned his head back.

Momma stealthily crept around the tree as the man urinated. She raised the sickle in her right hand and swung. The man heard momma's sickle cut the wind. His eyes opened wide as he looked down to the ground and saw his penis lying there. Blood gushed from the wound where his penis was once attached. In shock, he attempted to scream, but nothing came out. He fell to his knees and placed both of his hands on the wound, trying to stop the blood from flowing so quickly from it. Momma watched stoically as the tall man bled out. He fell at momma's feet, attempting to ask for mercy. Momma lifted her right foot into the air as high as she could and stomped his face completely in.

At that moment, the burly man who was just talking to the tall man noticed he had not returned. He turned to the other men in the lean-to, who were sipping coffee from their tin cups.

"Hey! More than a minute to pee, means you playin' with it, right?" He laughed, as well as the others. The burly man called out to the tall one,

"Hey! Did you here me, boy? Let that thang be. It'll be taken care of directly!" He giggled and waited for a response, but there wasn't one.

Concerned and curious, he stood and walked outside of the lean-to. He looked in the direction the tall man had walked. Rain pelted him in the face, so he squinted to get a better look around. Looking in the direction of the large tree, he saw the tall man's motionless body on the ground. He pulled his pistol immediately and scanned the camp, turning his head to the others and softly muttered, "Hey you sons-a-bitches be quiet in there. We got company!"

The other men came running out of the lean-to with their muskets and pistols pulled. The burly man placed his fingers to his lips telling the others to be quiet. He motioned with his pistol hand for them to spread out and circle the camp. The men nervously complied, spreading out through the camp.

The burly man walked cautiously over to the tall man's body and turned him over; his face frozen with terror. He felt a cold chill run down his spine as he backed away from the tall man's body. Suddenly, the burly man turned, and through reflex action, fired his pistol into the ground, as he fell down. Bo Daddy ran quickly to the burly man's body, pulled his knife from his temple, and disappeared once again into the woods. Bishop's remaining men in the camp shot their weapons in every direction hitting nothing. Once empty they attempted to reload their weapons. That is when momma came running and screaming out of the woods toward the remaining six men. She jumped and kicked the first, who was fumbling with his weapon, trying to reload his musket. He flew backward and fell into a large puddle of muddy water. Then she ran through the gauntlet of men, slashing the second man's throat with the sickle in her left hand. Then, spun to her right and hit another with blindingly fast right and left sickle strikes down the right side of his body, as if she was playing the drum. His body contorted with each blow. On the next three, she attacked their lower extremities, two on her left and one on her right.

The men abandoned trying to reload their weapons; momma was too fast. They dropped their muskets and pulled their knives. The first man on the right swung his large blade at momma, and missed her by a hair. Momma chopped the second man on the right's legs up with her sickles. He screamed in agony as he fell to the ground grabbing his right leg, which was nearly severed and hanging together by only a strip of skin.

Momma continued to attack bellow the men's waists, sticking the sickle in her left hand into the genitals of the second man on the left, then, cut his throat with the sickle in her right hand for good measure. He fell to the ground with blood gushing from his throat. Blood splattered all over her.

She jumped toward the fifth man, hitting the buttons on her new sickles, which allowed her to flip the blades back for punching. Momma leaped through the air, hitting the ground in front of him. Like a cat, she rolled forward and athletically jumped to her feet in front of him. He swung a right hook at momma, which she blocked with her left arm, causing him to cut his arm on her blade that is now positioned on her forearm. The fifth man groaned in pain as he swung a left at momma. She blocked his left as well with her right arm, cutting his arm again. Momma gathered herself and threw a flurry of punches into the face and body of the fifth man; every punch she threw opened a new wound, spraying blood into the air, and into her face. A bloody mess, he fell backward to the ground. Momma, like a crazed animal, leapt onto his body and continued punching him repeatedly.

The sixth man watched as momma pounded his comrade over, and over, again. Seeing an opportunity, he crept up behind momma, pulled his pistol and aimed it at her. Between one of her punches, momma heard what sounded like a hammer smashing a grapefruit. She turned her head quickly in the direction of the sound. She turned in time to see the sixth man lowering his pistol and falling to the ground with a thud. One of Bilali's hammers was lodged in his skull.

Bilali stepped from behind a tree, not far from where the sixth man had fallen. He walked over to the sixth man's body and pulled his hammer from the man's head. He nodded to momma respectfully. Momma nodded back. He walked over to momma and grabbed her under her arm, to help her to her feet.

The first man momma kicked when she attacked the camp, finally came to and leaped to his feet, terrified. He ran towards the woods as fast as his legs would take him. He successfully made it to the tree line surrounding the camp. Periodically looking behind himself, making sure momma was not on his tail.

Without warning, Bo Daddy stepped calmly from behind a large Georgia Pine and stuck a knife into the first man's abdomen. His eyes widened and the expression of disbelief came over his face. He looked into Bo Daddy's eyes, begging for mercy. Bo Daddy smiled at him, and began to stab him as deep as his knife would go repeatedly, until the man fell backwards to the ground.

Bo Daddy, hand totally covered in blood,

pulled his knife from the man's stomach and wiped the blade off in the dead man's hair. He stood and walked to where momma and Bilali were standing. Bo Daddy looked at Bilali and spoke.

"Me glad to see ya, big brudda." Bilali smirked at Bo Daddy.

"It took I awhile, but I admit dis, brudda... Me was wrong." He and Bo Daddy gripped each other's forearm.

"No, we both are ta blame, brotha." Bo Daddy said with tears in his eyes. They embraced one another tightly. Momma looked on as Bo Daddy and Bilali made peace with one another.

Momma saw something move out of the corner of her eye. She scanned the surrounding woods suspiciously. Momma caught the reflection of the campfire on a musket barrel. She turned to warn Bo Daddy and Bilali, who were still embracing, but, before she could, the woods erupted with multiple musket fire, from point blank range. Sparks flew off Bilali's breastplate, knocking him to the ground.

Bo Daddy dove to the ground and rolled

over. He jumped to his feet and sprung behind a tree. With both hands on his stomach, he slid his back down the trunk of the tree until he was sitting on the ground. Bo Daddy slowly removed his hand from his stomach and blood gushed from his abdomen. He looked into the sky and laughed-- realizing his wound was mortal.

Momma zigzagged as she sprinted through the camp, avoiding the dozens of minie balls flying through the air. She could hear them whizzing past her head. She dove behind a large rock and got as low as she could. Bishop yelled to her mockingly. "Nancy, honey! I'm home! Baby, did you miss me? Oh yeah, I bought a few more boys with me. Say hello, boys!" The woods once again erupted into gunfire.

Momma got as low as she could again, as the minie balls impact the front of the rock she was hiding behind and the trees around her. Bo Daddy, not far away, reached down and grabbed a handful of red-clay mud and placed it onto the wound in his belly to slow the bleeding. He crawled low, avoiding the gunfire.

Bishop smiled widely as his men fired upon momma and Bo Daddy. Dirty Sam stood bravely and began to move in on momma's position. He turned to the others and shouted, "Come on, boys! I ain't a-scared of no nigger bitch! Let's go!" His friends stood too and began to move in as well.

Bo Daddy crawled over to the rock momma was hiding behind. His condition weakened by severe blood loss. Momma half smiled at him. "Where you been, Bo? I feared you was dead." Bo Daddy laughed, then coughed up blood. He rolled over and showed momma his terrible wound. Momma got choked up when she saw how severe it was.

"Oh, Bo, what have I done to you? I'm sorry for getting you into this..." Bo Daddy struggled to lift himself up against the rock next to momma. "Dat's nonsense, gal. You brought I and me brudda back ta gedder again. Bein' wit cha, has been me life's blessin." Bo Daddy removed his favorite two knives from his vest and took one in each hand. He looked over at momma and smiled with blood-stained teeth. "Now, let us finish dis ting."

Momma smiled back at him and flipped her weapons back into traditional sickle position.

She turned her head to Bo Daddy.

"Bo Daddy?"

"Yeah, gal.", he answered, wiping blood from his mouth with the back of his hand.

"I never told you this, but I..." Bo Daddy interrupted.

"Me already know, gal. Me already know." Momma smiled while fighting back tears. She nodded her head and breathed deeply, before she and Bo Daddy jumped from behind the rock together.

Bo Daddy was hit instantly by multiple minie balls. Blood shot out of his body with each impact. Through the blood and smoke in his eyes, he saw Dirty Sam approaching. Bo Daddy gathered himself, summoning the last of his strength and concentration. With his last act on this earth, he threw the knife into Dirty Sam's throat, who dropped his pistol, and grabbed his throat as he fell to the ground in disbelief.

Momma watched as her beloved Bo Daddy fell to the ground with his eyes wide open. At that very moment, Bishop stood and took careful aim at momma. She lifted her head and saw him. With no concern for herself, she turned and screamed as she ran toward him.

"Aiyeee!"

Momma was fired upon from all sides. Her focus was solely on Bishop. It was almost as if she could not feel the metal balls ripping through her body. Her hatred of him was so great the minie balls could not even stop her momentum. Bishop looked up from his musket sight and marveled at momma running through the hail of minie balls. For a split second, he took pride in the fact that his family had created such a fine warrior. He put his eye back onto the sight of his musket.

Momma summoned the last of her strength leaping into the air toward Bishop. He fired his musket, ripping another hole in momma's chest. She lifted her right arm and with one last mighty swing, cut Bishop in half, from his left shoulder, to just below his chest. He fell to the ground almost in pieces, literally. Momma was bleeding from her mouth and had minie ball wounds everywhere. She looked into the sky, closed her eyes and cried out,

"Ruuuuuubby!"

END OF BOOK I

BLACK NANCY BOOK II: RISE OF RUBY
(FIRST PEEK)
CHAPTER 1

I Rise

I ran as fast as my legs would carry me through the woods that day-- towards the sound of the multiple muskets firing all at once. As I ducked and dodged the pine branches hanging over the sliver of pathway I was running on, the rain started to come down like buckets, quickly soaking my dress all the way through. I reached the tree line near the battle between momma and Bishop's men in time to see her running toward Bishop's position in the woods.

Slowly, I dropped to the ground watching as momma ran through a barrage of musket and pistol fire. Cringing, I covered my eyes as minie balls ripped through my momma's body. Some of the minie balls hit her and stayed inside of her body. Others passed right through. Still she advanced, seemingly impervious to pain. A strange feeling came over me as I watched this spectacle. I believe it was a combination of intense anguish, extreme anger, and immense pride.

Anguish, because as much as I didn't want to believe it, I knew my momma would not survive this battle. Angry, at the fact these crackas just wouldn't let us be. They had taken our freedom, our bodies, and every strand of self-respect, and that still wasn't enough! But also pride, in the way my mother, in the face of certain death, was brave enough and willing to die for what she believed in.

In that moment, the only thing I was sure of, was that I would no longer be a spectator in this battle for my peoples' freedom. I was no longer the little girl who escaped bondage, being protected by her mother. These very same men had stolen my innocence, just the day before. These horrible, wicked men... stealing my momma's breath away from her right before my eyes.

Gritting my teeth with my eyes shut tightly, I lifted my head allowing the steady rainfall to cascade down my face. It was to be my baptism; for I swore to become the women my momma raised and trained me to be, right then!

ↀ

ABOUT THE AUTHOR

Lennox Nelson, a proud native of South Philadelphia and alumnus of Syracuse University. Nelson's vast experiences, from his world travels, has enriched his life with future stories to be told. Some of which come to life in the BLACK NANCY series. Lennox and his wife, Beverly, reside in the Washington DC area.

Visit https://www.facebook.com/BlackNancyFanClub where the fans of BLACK NANCY come to discuss, receive specials and to find out the release date for BLACK NANCY BOOK II: RISE OF RUBY.

Made in the USA
San Bernardino, CA
25 September 2015